PENGUIN BOOKS

THE GREEN MILE: PART 6
COFFEY ON THE MILE

Stephen King, one of the world's bestselling writers, was born in Portland, Maine, in 1947, and was educated at the University of Maine at Orono. He shot to fame with the publication of his first novel, *Carrie*, and his subsequent titles include *The Shining* and *Misery*, which have all been made into highly successful films. He lives with his wife, the novelist Tabitha King, and their three children in Bangor, Maine.

Stephen King's *Rose Madder* is out now from New English Library. His new novel, *Desperation*, is coming shortly in hardback from Hodder & Stoughton.

The Green Mile is a novel of six parts, comprising: *The Two Dead Girls*, *The Mouse on the Mile*, *Coffey's Hands*, *The Bad Death of Eduard Delacroix*, *Night Journey* and *Coffey on the Mile*. All six volumes are published in Penguin.

ALSO BY STEPHEN KING

Novels
Carrie   Salem's Lot   The Shining
The Stand   The Dead Zone   Firestarter
Cujo   The Dark Tower: The Gunslinger   Christine
Pet Sematary   Cycle of the Werewolf
The Talisman (*with Peter Straub*)
It   Eyes of the Dragon   Misery
The Tommyknockers
The Dark Tower II: The Drawing of the Three
The Dark Tower III: The Waste Lands
The Dark Half   Needful Things   Gerald's Game
Dolores Claiborne   Insomnia
Rose Madder

As Richard Bachman
Rage   The Long Walk   Roadwork
The Running Man   Thinner

Collections
Night Shift   Different Seasons   Skeleton Crew
Four Past Midnight   Nightmares and Dreamscapes

Non-Fiction
Danse Macabre

Screenplays
Creepshow   Cat's Eye   Silver Bullet
Maximum   Overdrive   Pet Sematary
Golden Years   Sleepwalkers   The Stand

STEPHEN KING

The Green Mile

PART SIX

Coffey on the Mile

PENGUIN BOOKS

PENGUIN BOOKS

Published by the Penguin Group
Penguin Books Ltd, 27 Wrights Lane, London W8 5TZ, England
Penguin Books USA Inc., 375 Hudson Street, New York, New York 10014, USA
Penguin Books Australia Ltd, Ringwood, Victoria, Australia
Penguin Books Canada Ltd, 10 Alcorn Avenue, Toronto, Ontario, Canada M4V 3B2
Penguin Books (NZ) Ltd, 182–190 Wairau Road, Auckland 10, New Zealand

Penguin Books Ltd, Registered Offices: Harmondsworth, Middlesex, England

Published simultaneously in the USA in Signet and
in Great Britain in Penguin Books 1996
1 3 5 7 9 10 8 6 4 2

Printed in England by Clays Ltd, St Ives plc

1

I sat in the Georgia Pines sunroom, my father's fountain pen in my hand, and time was lost to me as I recalled the night Harry and Brutal and I took John Coffey off the Mile and to Melinda Moores, in an effort to save her life. I wrote about the drugging of William Wharton, who fancied himself the second coming of Billy the Kid; I wrote of how we stuck Percy in the straitjacket and jugged him in the restraint room at the end of the Green Mile; I wrote about our strange night journey—both terrifying and exhilarating—and the miracle that befell at the end of it. We saw John Coffey drag a woman back, not just from the edge of her grave, but from what seemed to us to be the very bottom of it.

I wrote and was very faintly aware of the Georgia Pines version of life going on around me. Old folks went down to supper, then trooped off to the Resource Center (yes, you are permitted a chuckle) for their evening dose of network sitcoms. I seem to remember my friend Elaine bringing me a sandwich, and thanking her, and eating it, but I couldn't tell you what time of the evening she brought it, or what was in it. Most of me was back in 1932, when our sandwiches were usually bought off old Toot-Toot's rolling gospel snack-wagon, cold pork a nickel, corned beef a dime.

I remember the place quieting down as the relics who live here made ready for another night of thin and troubled sleep; I heard Mickey—maybe not the best orderly in the place, but certainly the kindest— singing "Red River Valley" in his good tenor as he went around dispensing the evening meds: *"From this valley they say you are going . . . We will miss your bright eyes and sweet smile . . ."* The song made me think of Melinda again, and what she had said to John after the miracle had happened. *I dreamed of you. I dreamed you were wandering in the dark, and so was I. We found each other.*

Georgia Pines grew quiet, midnight came and passed, and still I wrote. I got to Harry reminding us that, even though we had gotten John back to the prison without being discovered, we still had Percy waiting for us. "The evening ain't over as long as we got him to contend with" is more or less what Harry said.

That's where my long day of driving my father's pen at last caught up with me. I put it down—just for a few seconds, I thought, so I could flex some life back into the fingers—and then I put my forehead down on my arm and closed my eyes to rest them. When I opened them again and raised my head, morning sun glared in at me through the windows. I looked at my watch and saw it was past eight. I had slept, head on arms like an old drunk, for what must have been six hours. I got up, wincing, trying to stretch some life into my back. I thought about going down to the kitchen, getting some toast, and going for my morning walk, then looked down at the sheafs of scribbled pages scattered across the desk. All at once I decided to put off the walk for awhile. I had a chore, yes, but it could keep, and I didn't feel like playing hide-and-seek with Brad Dolan that morning.

Instead of walking, I'd finish my story. Sometimes it's better to push on through, no matter how much your mind and body may protest. Sometimes it's the only way to *get* through. And what I remember most about that morning is how desperately I wanted to get free of John Coffey's persistent ghost.

"Okay," I said. "One more mile. But first . . ."

I walked down to the toilet at the end of the second-floor hall. As I stood inside there, urinating, I happened to glance up at the smoke detector on the ceiling. That made me think of Elaine, and how she had distracted Dolan so I could go for my walk and do my little chore the day before. I finished peeing with a grin on my face.

I walked back to the sunroom, feeling better (and a *lot* comfier in my nether regions). Someone—Elaine, I have no doubt—had set down a pot of tea beside my pages. I drank greedily, first one cup, then another, before I even sat down. Then I resumed my place, uncapped the fountain pen, and once more began to write.

I was just slipping fully into my story when a shadow fell on me. I looked up and felt a sinking in my stomach. It was Dolan, standing between me and the windows. He was grinning.

"Missed you going on your morning walk, Paulie," he said, "so I thought I'd come and see what you were up to. Make sure you weren't, you know, sick."

"You're all heart and a mile wide," I said. My voice sounded all right—so far, anyway—but my heart was pounding hard. I was afraid of him, and I don't think that realization was entirely new. He reminded me of Percy Wetmore, and I'd never been afraid of *him* ... but when I knew Percy, I had been young.

Brad's smile widened, but became no less pleasant.

"Folks tellin me you been in here all night, Paulie, just writing your little report. Now, that's just no good. Old farts like you need their beauty rest."

"Percy—" I began, then saw a frown crease his grin and realized my mistake. I took a deep breath and began again. "Brad, what have you got against me?"

He looked puzzled for a moment, maybe a bit un-settled. Then the grin returned. "Old-timer," he said, "could be I just don't like your face. What you writin, anyway? Last will n testicles?"

He came forward, craning. I slapped my hand over the page I'd been working on. The rest of them I began to rake together with my free hand, crumpling some in my hurry to get them under my arm and under cover.

"Now," he said, as if speaking to a baby, "that ain't going to work, you old sweetheart. If Brad wants to look, Brad is going to look. And you can take that to the everfucking *bank*."

His hand, young and hideously strong, closed over my wrist, and squeezed. Pain sank into my hand like teeth, and I groaned.

"Let go," I managed.

"When you let me see," he replied, and he was no longer smiling. His face was cheerful, though; the kind of good cheer you only see on the faces of folks who enjoy being mean. "Let me see, Paulie. I want to know what you're writing." My hand began to move away from the top page. From our trip with John back through the tunnel under the road. "I want to see if it has anything to do with where you—"

"Let that man alone."

The voice was like a harsh whipcrack on a dry, hot day ... and the way Brad Dolan jumped, you would have thought his ass had been the target. He let go of my hand, which thumped back down on my paperwork, and we both looked toward the door.

Elaine Connelly was standing there, looking fresh and stronger than she had in days. She wore jeans that showed off her slim hips and long legs; there was a blue ribbon in her hair. She had a tray in her arthritic hands—juice, a scrambled egg, toast, more tea. And her eyes were blazing.

"What do you think you're doing?" Brad asked. "He can't eat up here."

"He can, and he's going to," she said in that same dry tone of command. I had never heard it before, but I welcomed it now. I looked for fear in her eyes and saw not a speck—only rage. "And what you're going to do is get out of here before you go beyond the cockroach level of nuisance to that of slightly larger vermin—*Rattus Americanus,* let us say."

He took a step toward her, looking both unsure of himself and absolutely furious. I thought it a dangerous combination, but Elaine didn't flinch as he approached. "I bet I know who set off that goddam smoke alarm," Dolan said. "Might could have been a certain old bitch with claws for hands. Now get out of here. Me and Paulie haven't finished our little talk, yet."

"His name is *Mr. Edgecombe,*" she said, "and if I ever hear you call him Paulie again, I think I can promise you that your days of employment here at Georgia Pines will end, Mr. Dolan."

"Just who do you think you are?" he asked her. He was hulking over her, now, trying to laugh and not quite making it.

"I think," she said calmly, "that I am the grandmother of the man who is currently Speaker of the Georgia House of Representatives. A man who loves his relatives, Mr. Dolan. Especially his *older* relatives."

The effortful smile dropped off his face the way that writing comes off a blackboard swiped with a wet sponge. I saw uncertainty, the possibility that he was being bluffed, the fear that he was not, and a certain dawning logical assumption: it would be easy enough to check, she must know that, ergo she was telling the truth.

Suddenly I began to laugh, and although the sound was rusty, it was right. I was remembering how many times Percy Wetmore had threatened us with his connections, back in the bad old days. Now, for the first time in my long, long life, such a threat was being made again . . . but this time it was being made on my behalf.

Brad Dolan looked at me, glaring, then looked back at her.

"I mean it," Elaine said. "At first I thought I'd just let you be—I'm old, and that seemed easiest. But when my friends are threatened and abused, I *do not* just let be. Now get out of here. And without one more word."

His lips moved like those of a fish—oh, how badly he wanted to say that one more word (perhaps the one that rhymes with *witch*). He didn't, though. He gave me a final look, and then strode past her and out into the hall.

I let out my breath in a long, ragged sigh as Elaine set the tray down in front of me and then set herself down across from me. "Is your grandson really Speaker of the House?" I asked.

"He really is."

"Then what are you doing here?"

"Speaker of the statehouse makes him powerful enough to deal with a roach like Brad Dolan, but it doesn't make him *rich,*" she said, laughing. "Besides, I like it here. I like the company."

"I will take that as a compliment," I said, and I did.

"Paul, are you all right? You look so tired." She reached across the table and brushed my hair away from my forehead and eyebrows. Her fingers were twisted, but her touch was cool and wonderful. I closed my eyes for a moment. When I opened them again, I had made a decision.

"I'm all right," I said. "And almost finished. Elaine, would you read something?" I offered her the pages I had clumsily swept together. They were probably no longer in the right order—Dolan really had scared me badly—but they were numbered and she could quickly put them right.

She looked at me consideringly, not taking what I was offering. Yet, anyway. "Are you done?"

"It'll take you until afternoon to read what's there," I said. "If you can make it out at all, that is."

Now she *did* take the pages, and looked down at them. "You write with a very fine hand, even when that hand is obviously tired," she said. "I'll have no trouble with this."

"By the time you finish reading, I will have finished writing," I said. "You can read the rest in a half an hour or so. And then . . . if you're still willing . . . I'd like to show you something."

"Is it to do with where you go most mornings and afternoons?"

I nodded.

She sat thinking about it for what seemed a long time, then nodded herself and got up with the pages in her hand. "I'll go out back," she said. "The sun is very warm this morning."

"And the dragon's been vanquished," I said. "This time by the lady fair."

She smiled, bent, and kissed me over the eyebrow in the sensitive place that always makes me shiver. "We'll hope so," she said, "but in my experience, dragons like Brad Dolan are hard to get rid of." She hesitated. "Good luck, Paul. I hope you can vanquish whatever it is that has been festering in you."

"I hope so, too," I said, and thought of John Coffey. *I couldn't help it*, John had said. *I tried, but it was too late*.

I ate the eggs she'd brought, drank the juice, and pushed the toast aside for later. Then I picked up my pen and began to write again, for what I hoped would be the last time.

One last mile.

A green one.

2

When we brought John back to E Block that night, the gurney was a necessity instead of a luxury. I very much doubt if he could have made it the length of the tunnel on his own; it takes more energy to walk at a crouch than it does upright, and it was a damned low ceiling for the likes of John Coffey. I didn't like to think of him collapsing down there. How would we explain that, on top of trying to explain why we had dressed Percy in the madman's dinner-jacket and tossed him in the restraint room?

But we had the gurney—thank God—and John Coffey lay on it like a beached whale as we pushed him back to the storage-room stairs. He got down off it, staggered, then simply stood with his head lowered, breathing harshly. His skin was so gray he looked as if he'd been rolled in flour. I thought he'd be in the infirmary by noon . . . if he wasn't dead by noon, that was.

Brutal gave me a grim, desperate look. I gave it right back. "We can't carry him up, but we can help him," I said. "You under his right arm, me under his left."

"What about me?" Harry asked.

"Walk behind us. If he looks like going over backward, shove him forward again."

"And if that don't work, kinda crouch down where you think he's gonna land and soften the blow," Brutal said.

"Gosh," Harry said thinly, "you oughta go on the Orpheum Circuit, Brute, that's how funny *you* are."

"I got a sense of humor, all right," Brutal admitted.

In the end, we did manage to get John up the stairs. My biggest worry was that he might faint, but he didn't. "Go around me and check to make sure the storage room's empty," I gasped to Harry.

"What should I say if it's not?" Harry asked, squeezing under my arm. " 'Avon calling,' and then pop back in here?"

"Don't be a wisenheimer," Brutal said.

Harry eased the door open a little way and poked his head through. It seemed to me that he stayed that way for a very long time. At last he pulled back, looking almost cheerful. "Coast's clear. And it's *quiet*."

"Let's hope it stays that way," Brutal said. "Come on, John Coffey, almost home."

He was able to cross the storage room under his own power, but we had to help him up the three steps to my office and then almost push him through the little door. When he got to his feet again, he was breathing stertorously, and his eyes had a glassy sheen. Also—I noticed this with real horror—the right side of his mouth had pulled down, making it look like Melinda's had, when we walked into her room and saw her propped up on her pillows.

Dean heard us and came in from the desk at the head of the Green Mile. "Thank God! I thought you were never coming back, I'd half made up my mind you were caught, or the Warden plugged you, or—" He broke off, really seeing John for the first time. "Holy cats, what's wrong with him? He looks like he's dying!"

"He's not dying . . . are you, John?" Brutal said. His eyes flashed Dean a warning.

"Course not, I didn't mean actually *dyin*"—Dean gave a nervous little laugh—"but, jeepers . . ."

"Never mind," I said. "Help us get him back to his cell."

Once again we were foothills surrounding a mountain, but now it was a mountain that had suffered a few million years' worth of erosion, one that was blunted and sad. John Coffey moved slowly, breathing through his mouth like an old man who smoked too much, but at least he moved.

"What about Percy?" I asked. "Has he been kicking up a ruckus?"

"Some at the start," Dean said. "Trying to yell through the tape you put over his mouth. Cursing, I believe."

"Mercy me," Brutal said. "A good thing our tender ears were elsewhere."

"Since then, just a mulekick at the door every once in awhile, you know." Dean was so relieved to see us that he was babbling. His glasses slipped down to the end of his nose, which was shiny with sweat, and he pushed them back up. We passed Wharton's cell. That worthless young man was flat on his back, snoring like a sousaphone. His eyes were shut this time, all right.

Dean saw me looking and laughed.

"No trouble from that guy! Hasn't moved since he laid back down on his bunk. Dead to the world. As for Percy kicking the door every now and then, I never minded that a bit. Was glad of it, tell you the truth. If he didn't make any noise at all, I'd start wonderin if he hadn't choked to death on that gag you slapped over his cakehole. But that's not the best. You know the best? It's been as quiet as Ash Wednesday morning in New Orleans! Nobody's been down all night!" He said this last in a triumphant, gloating voice. "We got away with it, boys! We did!"

That made him think of why we'd gone through the whole comedy in the first place, and he asked about Melinda.

"She's fine," I said. We had reached John's cell. What Dean had said was just starting to sink in: *We got away with it, boys . . . we did.*

"Was it like . . . you know . . . the mouse?" Dean asked. He glanced briefly at the empty cell where Delacroix had lived with Mr. Jingles, then down at the restraint room, which had been the mouse's seeming point of origin. His voice dropped, the way people's voices do when they enter a big church where even the silence seems to whisper. "Was it a . . ." He gulped. "Shoot, you know what I mean— was it a miracle?"

The three of us looked at each other briefly, confirming what we already knew. "Brought her back from her damn grave is what he did," Harry said. "Yeah, it was a miracle, all right."

Brutal opened the double locks on the cell, and gave John a gentle push inside. "Go on, now, big boy. Rest awhile. You earned it. We'll just settle Percy's hash—"

"He's a bad man," John said in a low, mechanical voice.

"That's right, no doubt, wicked as a warlock," Brutal agreed in his most soothing voice, "but don't you worry a smidge about him, we're not going to let him near you. You just ease down on that bunk of yours and I'll have that cup of coffee to you in no time. Hot and strong. You'll feel like a new man."

John sat heavily on his bunk. I thought he'd fall back on it and roll to the wall as he usually did, but he just sat there for the time being, hands clasped loosely between his knees, head lowered, breathing hard through his mouth. The St. Christopher's medal Melinda had given him had fallen out of the top of his shirt and swung back and forth in the air. He'll keep you safe, that's what she'd told him, but John Coffey didn't look a bit safe. He looked like he had taken Melinda's place on the lip of that grave Harry had spoken of.

But I couldn't think about John Coffey just then.

I turned around to the others. "Dean, get Percy's pistol and hickory stick."

"Okay." He went back up to the desk, unlocked the drawer with the gun and the stick in it, and brought them back.

"Ready?" I asked them. My men—good men, and I was never prouder of them than I was that night—nodded. Harry and Dean both looked nervous; Brutal as stolid as ever. "Okay. I'm going to do the talking. The less the rest of you open your mouths, the better it'll probably be and the quicker it'll probably wrap up ... for better or worse. Okay?"

They nodded again. I took a deep breath and walked down to the Green Mile restraint room.

Percy looked up, squinting, when the light fell on him. He was sitting on the floor and licking at the tape I had slapped across his mouth. The part I'd wound around to the back of his head had come free (probably the sweat and brilliantine in his hair had loosened it), and he'd gotten a ways toward getting the rest off, as well. Another hour and he would've been bawling for help at the top of his lungs.

He used his feet to shove himself a little way backward when we came in, then stopped, no doubt realizing that there was nowhere to go except for the southeast corner of the room.

I took his gun and stick from Dean and held them out in Percy's direction. "Want these back?" I asked.

He looked at me warily, then nodded his head.

"Brutal," I said. "Harry. Get him on his feet."

They bent, hooked him under the canvas arms of the straitjacket, and up he came. I moved toward him until we were almost nose to nose. I could smell the sour sweat in which he'd been basting. Some of it probably came from his efforts to get free of the quiet-down coat, or to administer the occasional kicks to the door Dean had heard, but I thought most of his sweat had come as a result of plain old fear: fear of what we might do to him when we came back.

I'll be okay, they ain't *killers,* Percy would think . . . and then, maybe, he'd think of Old Sparky and it would cross his mind that yes, in a way we *were* killers. I'd done seventy-seven myself, more than any of the men I'd ever put the chest-strap on, more than Sergeant York himself got credit for in World War I. Killing Percy wouldn't be logical, but we'd already behaved illogically, he would have told himself as he sat there with his arms behind him, working with his tongue to get the tape off his mouth. And besides, logic most likely doesn't have much power over a person's thoughts when that person is sitting on the floor of a room with soft walls, wrapped up as neat and tight as any spider ever wrapped a fly.

Which is to say, if I didn't have him where I wanted now, I never would.

"I'll take the tape off your mouth if you promise not to start yowling," I said. "I want to have a talk with you, not a shouting match. So what do you say? Will you be quiet?"

I saw relief come up in his eyes as he realized that, if I wanted to talk, he really did stand a good chance of getting out of this with a whole skin. He nodded his head.

"If you start noising off, the tape goes back on," I said. "Do you understand that, too?"

Another nod, rather impatient this time.

I reached up, grabbed the end of the runner he'd worked loose, and gave it a hard yank. It made a loud peeling sound. Brutal winced. Percy yipped with pain and began rubbing his lips. He tried to speak, realized he couldn't do it with a hand over his mouth, and lowered it.

"Get me out of this nut-coat, you lugoon," he spat.

"In a minute," I said.

"Now! Now! Right n—"

I slapped his face. It was done before I'd even known I was going to do it . . . but of course I'd known it *might* come to that. Even back during the first talk about Percy that I'd had with Warden Moores, the one where Hal advised me to put Percy out for the Delacroix execution, I'd known it *might* come to that. A man's hand is like an animal that's only half-tame; mostly it's good, but sometimes it escapes and bites the first thing it sees.

The sound was a sharp *snap*, like a breaking branch. Dean gasped. Percy stared at me in utter shock, his eyes so wide they looked as if they must fall out of their sockets. His mouth opened and closed, opened and closed, like the mouth of a fish in an aquarium tank.

"Shut up and listen to me," I said. "You deserved to be punished for what you did to Del, and we gave you what you deserved. This was the only way we could do it. We all agreed, except for Dean, and he'll go along with us, because we'll make him sorry if he doesn't. Isn't that so, Dean?"

"Yes," Dean whispered. He was milk-pale. "Guess it is."

"And we'll make *you* sorry you were ever born," I went on. "We'll see that people know about how you sabotaged the Delacroix execution—"

"*Sabotaged—!*"

"—and how you almost got Dean killed. We'll blab enough to keep you out of almost any job your uncle can get you."

Percy was shaking his head furiously. He didn't believe that, perhaps *couldn't* believe that. My hand-print stood out on his pale cheek like a fortune-teller's sign.

"And no matter what, we'd see you beaten within an inch of your life. We wouldn't have to do it ourselves. We know people, too, Percy, are you so foolish you don't realize that? They aren't up in the state capital, but they still know how to legislate certain matters. These are people who have friends in here, people who have brothers in here, people who have fathers in here. They'd be happy to amputate the nose or the penis of a shitheels like you. They'd do it just so someone they care for could get an extra three hours in the exercise yard each week."

Percy had stopped shaking his head. Now he was only staring. Tears stood in his eyes, but didn't fall. I think they were tears of rage and frustration. Or maybe I just hoped they were.

"Okay—now look on the sunny side, Percy. Your lips sting a little from having the tape pulled off them, I imagine, but otherwise there's nothing hurt but your pride ... and nobody needs to know about that but the people in this room right now. And we'll never tell, will we, boys?"

They shook their heads. "Course not," Brutal said. "Green Mile business stays on the Green Mile. Always has."

"You're going on to Briar Ridge and we're going to leave you alone until you go," I said. "Do you want to leave it at that, Percy, or do you want to play hardball with us?"

There was a long, long silence as he considered—

I could almost see the wheels turning in his head as he tried out and rejected possible counters. And at last, I think a more basic truth must have overwhelmed the rest of his calculations: the tape was off his mouth, but he was still wearing the straitjacket and probably he had to piss like a racehorse.

"All right," he said. "We'll consider the matter closed. Now get me out of this coat. It feels like my shoulders are—"

Brutal stepped forward, shouldering me aside, and grabbed Percy's face with one big hand—fingers denting in Percy's right cheek, thumb making a deep dimple in his left.

"In a few seconds," he said. "First, you listen to me. Paul here is the big boss, and so he has to talk elegant sometimes."

I tried to remember anything elegant I might've said to Percy and couldn't come up with much. Still, I thought it might be best to keep my mouth shut; Percy looked suitably terrorized, and I didn't want to spoil the effect.

"People don't always understand that being elegant isn't the same as being soft, and that's where I come in. I don't worry about being elegant. I just say things straight out. So here it is, straight out: if you go back on your promise, we'll most likely take an ass-fucking. But then we'll find you—if we have to go all the way to Russia, we'll find you—and *we* will fuck *you*, not just up the ass but in every hole you own. We'll fuck you until you'll wish you were dead, and then we'll rub vinegar in the parts that are bleeding. Do you understand me?"

He nodded. With Brutal's hand digging into the soft sides of his face the way it was, Percy looked eerily like Old Toot-Toot.

Brutal let go of him and stepped back. I nodded to Harry, who went behind Percy and started unsnapping and unbuckling.

"Keep it in mind, Percy," Harry said. "Keep it in mind and let bygones be bygones."

All of it suitably scary, three bogeymen in bluesuits ... but I felt a kind of knowing despair sweep through me, all the same. He might keep quiet for a day or a week, continuing to calculate the odds on various actions, but in the end two things—his belief in his connections and his inability to walk away from a situation where he saw himself as the loser—would combine. When that happened, he would spill his guts. We had perhaps helped to save Melly Moores's life by taking John to her, and I wouldn't have changed that ("not for all the tea in China," as we used to say back in those days), but in the end we were going to hit the canvas and the ref was going to count us out. Short of murder, there was no way we could make Percy keep his end of the bargain, not once he was away from us and had started to get back what passed for his guts.

I took a little sidelong glance at Brutal and saw he knew this, too. Which didn't surprise me. There were no flies on Mrs. Howell's boy Brutus, never had been. He gave me a tiny shrug, just one shoulder lifting an inch and then dropping, but it was enough. *So what?* that shrug said. *What else is there, Paul? We did what we had to do, and we did it the best we could.*

Yes. Results hadn't been half-bad, either.

Harry undid the last buckle on the straitjacket. Grimacing with disgust and rage, Percy pawed it off and let it drop at his feet. He wouldn't look at any of us, not directly.

"Give me my gun and my baton," he said. I handed them over. He dropped the gun into its holster and shoved the hickory stick into its custom loop.

"Percy, if you think about it—"

"Oh, I intend to," he said, brushing past me. "I intend to think about it very hard. Starting right now. On my way home. One of you boys can clock me out at quitting time." He reached the door of the restraint room and turned to survey us with a look of angry, embarrassed contempt—a deadly combination for the secret we'd had some fool's hope of keeping.

"Unless, of course, you want to try explaining why I left early."

He left the room and went striding up the Green Mile, forgetting in his agitation why that green-floored central corridor was so wide. He had made this mistake once before and had gotten away with it. He would not get away with it again.

I followed him out the door, trying to think of a way to soothe him down—I didn't want him leaving E Block the way he was now, sweaty and dishevelled, with the red print of my hand still on his cheek. The other three followed me.

What happened then happened very fast—it was all over in no more than a minute, perhaps even less. Yet I remember all of it to this day—mostly, I think, because I told Janice everything when I got home and that set it in my mind. What happened afterward—the dawn meeting with Curtis Anderson, the inquest, the press-meeting Hal Moores set up for us (he was back by then, of course), and the eventual Board of Enquiry in the state capital—those things have blurred over the years like so much else in my memory. But as to what actually happened next there on the Green Mile, yes, that I remember perfectly well.

Percy was walking up the right side of the Mile with his head lowered, and I'll say this much: no ordinary prisoner could have reached him. John Coffey wasn't an ordinary prisoner, though. John Coffey was a giant, and he had a giant's reach.

I saw his long brown arms shoot out from between the bars and yelled, *"Watch it, Percy, watch it!"* Percy started to turn, his left hand dropping to the butt of his stick. Then he was seized and yanked against the front of John Coffey's cell, the right side of his face smashing into the bars.

He grunted and turned toward Coffey, raising the hickory club. John was certainly vulnerable to it; his own face was pressed so strenuously into the space between two of the center bars that he looked as if he was trying to squeeze his entire head through. It would have been impossible, of course, but that was how it looked. His right hand groped, found the nape of Percy's neck, curled around it, and yanked Percy's head forward. Percy brought the club down between the bars and onto John's temple. Blood flowed, but John paid no attention. His mouth pressed against Percy's mouth. I heard a whispering rush—an exhalatory sound, as of long-held breath. Percy jerked like a fish on a hook, trying to get away, but he never had a chance; John's right hand was pressed to the back of his neck, holding him firm. Their faces seemed to melt together, like the faces of lovers I have seen kissing passionately through bars.

Percy screamed, the sound muffled as it had been through the tape, and made another effort to pull back. For an instant their lips came apart a little, and I saw the black, swirling tide that was flowing out of John Coffey and into Percy Wetmore. What wasn't going into him through his quivering mouth was flowing in by way of his nostrils. Then the hand on the nape of his neck flexed, and Percy was pulled forward onto John's mouth again; was almost impaled on it.

Percy's left hand sprang open. His treasured hickory baton fell to the green linoleum. He never picked it up again.

I tried to lunge forward, I guess I *did* lunge forward, but my movements felt old and creaky to myself. I grabbed for my gun, but the strap was still across the burled-walnut grip, and at first I couldn't get it out of its holster. Beneath me, I seemed to feel the floor shake as it had in the back bedroom of the Warden's neat little Cape Cod. That I'm not sure of, but I know that one of the caged lightbulbs overhead broke. Fragments of glass showered down. Harry yelled in surprise.

At last I managed to thumb loose the safety strap over the butt of my .38, but before I could pull it out of its holster, John had thrust Percy away from him and stepped back into his cell. John was grimacing and rubbing his mouth, as if he had tasted something bad.

"What'd he do?" Brutal shouted. "What'd he do, Paul?"

"Whatever he took out of Melly, Percy's got it now," I said.

Percy was standing against the bars of Delacroix's old cell. His eyes were wide and blank—double zeros. I approached him carefully, expecting him to start coughing and choking the way John had after he'd finished with Melinda, but he didn't. At first he only stood there.

I snapped my fingers in front of his eyes. "Percy! Hey, Percy! Wake up!"

Nothing. Brutal joined me, and reached toward Percy's empty face with both hands.

"That isn't going to work," I said.

Ignoring me, Brutal clapped his hands sharply together twice, right in front of Percy's nose. And it *did* work, or appeared to work. His eyelids fluttered and he stared around—dazed, like someone hit over the head struggling back to consciousness. He looked from Brutal to me. All these years later, I'm pretty sure he didn't see either of us, but I thought he did then; I thought he was coming out of it.

He pushed away from the bars and swayed a little on his feet. Brutal steadied him. "Easy, boy, you all right?" Percy didn't answer, just stepped past Brutal and turned toward the duty desk. He wasn't staggering, exactly, but he was listing to port.

Brutal reached out for him. I pushed his hand away. "Leave him alone." Would I have said the same if I'd known what was going to happen next? I've asked myself that question a thousand times since the fall of 1932. There's never any answer.

Percy made twelve or fourteen paces, then stopped again, head lowered. He was outside of Wild Bill Wharton's cell by then. Wharton was still making those sousaphone noises. He slept through the whole thing. He slept through his own death, now that I think of it, which made him a lot luckier than most of the men who ended up here. Certainly luckier than he deserved.

Before we knew what was happening, Percy drew his gun, stepped to the bars of Wharton's cell, and emptied all six shots into the sleeping man. Just bam-bam-bam, bam-bam-bam, as fast as he could pull the trigger. The sound in that enclosed space was deafening; when I told Janice the story the next morning, I could still hardly hear the sound of my own voice for the ringing in my ears.

We ran at him, all four of us. Dean got there first— I don't know how, as he was behind Brutal and me when Coffey had hold of Percy—but he did. He grabbed Percy's wrist, prepared to wrestle the gun out of Percy's hand, but he didn't have to. Percy just let go, and the gun fell to the floor. His eyes went across us like they were skates and we were ice. There was a low hissing sound and a sharp ammoniac smell as Percy's bladder let go, then a *brrrap* sound and a thicker stink as he filled the other side of his pants, as well. His eyes had settled on a far corner of the corridor. They were eyes that never saw anything in this real world of ours again, so far as I know. Back near the beginning of this I wrote that Percy was at Briar Ridge by the time that Brutal found the colored slivers of Mr. Jingles's spool a couple of months later, and I didn't lie about that. He never got the office with the fan in the corner, though; never got a bunch of lunatic patients to push around, either. But I imagine he at least got his own private room.

He had connections, after all.

Wharton was lying on his side with his back against the wall of his cell. I couldn't see much then but a lot of blood soaking into the sheet and splattered across the cement, but the coroner said Percy had shot like Annie Oakley. Remembering Dean's story of how Percy had thrown his hickory baton at the mouse that time and barely missed, I wasn't too surprised. This time the range had been shorter and the target not moving. One in the groin, one in the gut, one in the chest, three in the head.

Brutal was coughing and waving at the haze of gunsmoke. I was coughing myself, but hadn't noticed it until then.

"End of the line," Brutal said. His voice was calm, but there was no mistaking the glaze of panic in his eyes.

I looked down the hallway and saw John Coffey sitting on the end of his bunk. His hands were clasped between his knees again, but his head was up and he no longer looked a bit sick. He nodded at me slightly, and I surprised myself—as I had on the day I offered him my hand—by returning the nod.

"What are we going to do?" Harry gibbered. "Oh Christ, what are we going to do?"

"Nothing we *can* do," Brutal said in that same calm voice. "We're hung. Aren't we, Paul?"

My mind had begun to move very fast. I looked at Harry and Dean, who were staring at me like scared kids. I looked at Percy, who was standing there with his hands and jaw dangling. Then I looked at my old friend, Brutus Howell.

"We're going to be okay," I said.

Percy at last commenced coughing. He doubled over, hands on his knees, almost retching. His face began to turn red. I opened my mouth, meaning to tell the others to stand back, but I never got a chance. He made a sound that was a cross between a dry-heave and a bullfrog's croak, opened his mouth, and spewed out a cloud of black, swirling stuff. It was so thick that for a moment we couldn't see his head. Harry said "Oh God save us" in a weak and watery voice. Then the stuff turned a white so dazzling it was like January sun on fresh snow. A moment later the cloud was gone. Percy straightened slowly up and resumed his vacant gaze down the length of the Green Mile.

"We didn't see that," Brutal said. "Did we, Paul?"

"No. I didn't and you didn't. Did you see it, Harry?"

"No," Harry said.

"Dean?"

"See what?" Dean took his glasses off and began to polish them. I thought he would drop them out of his trembling hands, but he managed not to.

" 'See what,' that's good. That's just the ticket. Now listen to your scoutmaster, boys, and get it right the first time, because time is short. It's a simple story. Let's not complicate it."

3

I told all this to Jan at around eleven o'clock that morning—*the next morning*, I almost wrote, but of course it was the same day. The longest one of my whole life, without a doubt. I told it pretty much as I have here, finishing with how William Wharton had ended up lying dead on his bunk, riddled with lead from Percy's sidearm.

No, that's not right. What I *actually* finished with was the stuff that came out of Percy, the bugs or the whatever-it-was. That was a hard thing to tell, even to your wife, but I told it.

As I talked, she brought me black coffee by the half-cup—at first my hands were shaking too badly to pick up a whole one without spilling it. By the time I finished, the shaking had eased some, and I felt that I could even take some food—an egg, maybe, or some soup.

"The thing that saved us was that we didn't really have to lie, any of us."

"Just leave a few things out," she said, and nodded. "Little things, mostly, like how you took a condemned murderer out of prison, and how he cured a dying woman, and how he drove that Percy Wetmore crazy by—what?—spitting a pureed brain tumor down his throat?"

"I don't know, Jan," I said. "I only know that if you keep talking like that, you'll end up either eating that soup yourself, or feeding it to the dog."

"I'm sorry. But I'm right, aren't I?"

"Yeah," I said. "Except we got away with the—" The what? You couldn't call it an escape, and furlough wasn't right, either. "—the field trip. Not even Percy can tell them about that, if he ever comes back."

"If he comes back," she echoed. "How likely is that?"

I shook my head to indicate I had no idea. But I did, actually; I didn't think he *was* going to come back, not in 1932, not in '42 or '52, either. In that I was right. Percy Wetmore stayed at Briar Ridge until it burned flat in 1944. Seventeen inmates were killed in that fire, but Percy wasn't one of them. Still silent and blank in every regard—the word I learned to describe that state is *catatonic*—he was led out by one of the guards long before the fire reached his wing. He went on to another institution—I don't remember the name and guess it doesn't matter, anyway—and died in 1965. So far as I know, the last time he ever spoke was when he told us we could clock him out at quitting time . . . unless we wanted to explain why he had left early.

The irony was that we never had to explain much of anything. Percy had gone crazy and shot William Wharton to death. That was what we told, and so far as it went, every word was true. When Anderson asked Brutal how Percy had seemed before the shooting and Brutal answered with one word—*"Quiet"*— I had a terrible moment when I felt that I might burst out laughing. Because that was true, too, Percy *had* been quiet, for most of his shift he'd had a swatch of friction-tape across his mouth and the best he'd been able to come up with was *mmmph, mmmph, mmmph.*

Curtis kept Percy there until eight o'clock, Percy as silent as a cigar-store Indian but a lot more eerie. By then Hal Moores had arrived, looking grim but competent, ready to climb back into the saddle. Curtis Anderson let him do just that, and with a sigh of relief the rest of us could almost hear. The bewildered, frightened old man was gone; it was the Warden who strode up to Percy, grabbed him by the shoulders with his big hands, and shook him hard.

"Son!" he shouted into Percy's blank face—a face that was already starting to soften like wax, I thought. *"Son!* Do you hear me? Talk to me if you hear me! I want to know what happened!"

Nothing from Percy, of course. Anderson wanted to get the Warden aside, discuss how they were going to handle it—it was a political hot potato if there had ever been one—but Moores put him off, at least for the time being, and drew me down the Mile. John Coffey was lying on his bunk with his face to the wall, legs dangling outrageously, as they always did. He appeared to be sleeping and probably was ... but he wasn't *always* what he appeared, as we had found out.

"Did what happened at my house have anything to do with what happened here when you got back?" Moores asked in a low voice. "I'll cover you as much as I can, even if it means my job, but I have to know."

I shook my head. When I spoke, I also kept my voice low-pitched. There were now almost a dozen screws milling around at the head of the aisle. Another was photographing Wharton in his cell. Curtis Anderson had turned to watch that, and for the time being, only Brutal was watching us. "No, sir. We got

John back into his cell just like you see, then let Percy out of the restraint room, where we'd stashed him for safekeeping. I thought he'd be hot under the collar, but he wasn't. Just asked for his sidearm and baton. He didn't say anything else, just walked off up the corridor. Then, when he got to Wharton's cell, he pulled his gun and started shooting."

"Do you think being in the restraint room . . . did something to his mind?"

"No, sir."

"Did you put him in the straitjacket?"

"No, sir. There was no need."

"He was quiet? Didn't struggle?"

"No struggle."

"Even when he saw you meant to put him in the restraint room, he was quiet and didn't struggle."

"That's right." I felt an urge to embroider on this—to give Percy at least a line or two—and conquered it. Simpler would be better, and I knew it. "There was no fuss. He just went over into one of the far corners and sat down."

"Didn't speak of Wharton then?"

"No, sir."

"Didn't speak of Coffey, either?"

I shook my head.

"Could Percy have been laying for Wharton? Did he have something against the man?"

"That might be," I said, lowering my voice even more. "Percy was careless about where he walked, Hal. One time Wharton reached out, grabbed him up against the bars, and messed him over some." I paused. "Felt him up, you could say."

"No worse than that? Just ... 'messed him over' ... and that was all?"

"Yes, but it was pretty bad for Percy, just the same. Wharton said something about how he'd rather screw Percy than Percy's sister."

"Um." Moores kept looking sideways at John Coffey, as if he needed constant reassurance that Coffey was a real person, actually in the world. "It doesn't explain what's happened to him, but it goes a good piece toward explaining why it was Wharton he turned on and not Coffey or one of you men. And speaking of your men, Paul, will they all tell the same story?"

"Yes, sir," I told him. "And they will," I said to Jan, starting in on the soup she brought to the table. "I'll see to it."

"You *did* lie," she said. "You lied to Hal."

Well, that's a wife for you, isn't it? Always poking around for moth-holes in your best suit, and finding one more often than not.

"I guess, if you want to look at it that way. I didn't tell him anything we both won't be able to live with, though. Hal's in the clear, I think. He wasn't even *there*, after all. He was home tending his wife until Curtis called him."

"Did he say how Melinda was?"

"Not then, there wasn't time, but we spoke again just as Brutal and I were leaving. Melly doesn't remember much, but she's fine. Up and walking. Talking about next year's flower beds."

My wife sat watching me eat for some little time. Then she asked, "Does Hal know it's a miracle, Paul? Does he understand that?"

"Yes. We all do, all of us that were there."

"Part of me wishes I'd been there, too," she said, "but I think most of me is glad I wasn't. If I'd seen the scales fall from Saul's eyes on the road to Damascus, I probably would have died of a heart attack."

"Naw," I said, tilting my bowl to capture the last spoonful, "probably would have cooked him some soup. This is pretty fine, hon."

"Good." But she wasn't really thinking about soup or cooking or Saul's conversion on the Damascus road. She was looking out the window toward the ridges, her chin propped on her hand, her eyes as hazy as those ridges look on summer mornings when it's going to be hot. Summer mornings like the one when the Detterick girls had been found, I thought for no reason. I wondered why they hadn't screamed.

Their killer had hurt them; there had been blood on the porch, and on the steps. So why hadn't they screamed?

"You think John Coffey really killed that man Wharton, don't you?" Janice asked, looking back from the window at last. "Not that it was an accident, or anything like that; you think he used Percy Wetmore on Wharton like a gun."

"Yes."

"Why?"

"I don't know."

"Tell me again about what happened when you took Coffey off the Mile, would you? Just that part."

So I did. I told her how the skinny arm shooting out from between the bars and grabbing John's bicep had reminded me of a snake—one of the water moccasins we were all scared of when we were kids swimming in the river—and how Coffey had said Wharton was a bad man. Almost whispering it.

"And Wharton said . . . ?" My wife was looking out the window again, but she was listening, all right.

"Wharton said, 'That's right, nigger, bad as you'd want.' "

"And that's all."

"Yes. I had a feeling that something was going to happen right then, but nothing did. Brutal took

Wharton's hand off John and told him to lie down, which Wharton did. He was out on his feet to start with. Said something about how niggers should have their own electric chair, and that was all. We went about our business."

"John Coffey called him a bad man."

"Yep. Said the same thing about Percy once, too. Maybe more than once. I can't remember exactly when, but I know he did."

"But Wharton never did anything to John Coffey personally, did he? Like he did to Percy, I mean."

"No. The way their cells were—Wharton up by the duty desk on one side, John down a ways on the other—they could hardly see each other."

"Tell me again how Coffey looked when Wharton grabbed him."

"Janice, this isn't getting us anywhere."

"Maybe it isn't and maybe it is. Tell me again how he looked."

I sighed. "I guess you'd have to say shocked. He gasped. Like you would if you were sunning at the beach and I snuck up and trickled a little cold water down your back. Or like he'd been slapped."

"Well, sure," she said. "Being grabbed out of no-where like that startled him, woke him up for a second."

"Yes," I said. And then, "No."

"Well which is it? Yes or no?"

"No. It wasn't being *startled*. It was like when he wanted me to come into his cell so he could cure my infection. Or when he wanted me to hand him the mouse. It was being surprised, but not by being touched . . . not *exactly*, anyway . . . oh Christ, Jan, I don't know."

"All right, we'll leave it," she said. "I just can't imagine why John did it, that's all. It's not as if he's violent by nature. Which leads to another question, Paul: how can you execute him if you're right about those girls? How can you possibly put him in the electric chair if someone else—"

I jerked in my chair. My elbow struck my bowl and knocked it off onto the floor, where it broke. An idea had come to me. It was more intuition than logic at that point, but it had a certain black elegance.

"Paul?" Janice asked, alarmed. "What's wrong?"

"I don't know," I said. "I don't know anything for sure, but I'm going to find out if I can."

4

The aftermath of the shooting was a three-ring circus, with the governor in one ring, the prison in another, and poor brain-blasted Percy Wetmore in the third. And the ringmaster? Well, the various gentlemen of the press took turns at that job. They weren't as bad then as they are now—they didn't *allow* themselves to be as bad—but even back then before Geraldo and Mike Wallace and the rest of them, they could gallop along pretty good when they really got the bit in their teeth. That was what happened this time, and while the show lasted, it was a good one.

But even the liveliest circus, the one with the scariest freaks, funniest clowns, and wildest animals, has to leave town eventually. This one left after the Board of Enquiry, which sounds pretty special and fearsome, but actually turned out to be pretty tame and perfunctory. Under other circumstances, the governor undoubtedly would have demanded someone's head on a platter, but not this time. His nephew by marriage—his wife's own blood kin—had gone crackers and killed a man. Had killed a killer—there was that, at least, and thank God for it—but Percy had still shot the man as he lay sleeping in his cell, which was not quite sporting. When you added in the fact that the young man in question remained just as mad as a March hare, you could understand why the governor only wanted it to go away, and as soon as possible.

Our trip to Warden Moores's house in Harry Terwilliger's truck never came out. The fact that Percy had been straitjacketed and locked in the restraint room during the time we were away never came out. The fact that William Wharton had been doped to the gills when Percy shot him never came out, either. Why would it? The authorities had no reason to suspect anything in Wharton's system but half a dozen slugs. The coroner removed those, the mortician put him in a pine box, and that was the end of the man with *Billy the Kid* tattooed on his left forearm. Good riddance to bad rubbish, you might say.

All in all, the uproar lasted about two weeks. During that time I didn't dare fart sideways, let alone take a day off to investigate the idea I'd gotten at my kitchen table on the morning after all the upheavals. I knew for sure that the circus had left town when I got to work on a day just shy of the middle of November—the twelfth, I think, but don't hold me to that. That was the day I found the piece of paper I'd been dreading on the middle of my desk: the DOE on John Coffey. Curtis Anderson had signed it instead of Hal Moores, but of course it was just as legal either way, and of course it had needed to go through Hal in order to get to me. I could imagine Hal sitting at his desk in Administration with that piece of paper in his hand, sitting there and thinking of his wife, who had become something of a nine days' wonder to the doctors at Indianola General Hospital. She'd had her own DOE papers handed to her by those doctors, but John Coffey had torn them up. Now, however, it was Coffey's turn to walk the Green Mile, and who among us could stop it? Who among us *would* stop it?

The date on the death warrant was November 20th. Three days after I got it—the fifteenth, I think—I had Janice call me in sick. A cup of coffee later I was driving north in my badly sprung but otherwise reliable Ford. Janice had kissed me on my way and wished me good luck; I'd thanked her but no longer had any clear idea what good luck would be—finding what I was looking for or not finding it. All I knew for sure is that I didn't feel much like singing as I drove. Not that day.

By three that afternoon I was well up in the ridge country. I got to the Purdom County Courthouse just before it closed, looked at some records, then had a visit from the Sheriff, who had been informed by the county clerk that a stranger was poking in amongst the local skeletons. Sheriff Catlett wanted to know what I thought I was doing. I told him. Catlett thought it over and then told me something interesting. He said he'd deny he'd ever said a word if I spread it around, and it wasn't conclusive anyway, but it was something, all right. It was sure something. I thought about it all the way home, and that night there was a lot of thinking and precious little sleeping on my side of the bed.

The next day I got up while the sun was still just a rumor in the east and drove downstate to Trapingus County. I skirted around Homer Cribus, that great bag of guts and waters, speaking to Deputy Sheriff Rob McGee instead. McGee didn't want to hear what I was telling him. Most vehemently didn't want to hear it. At one point I was pretty sure he was going to punch me in the mouth so he could *stop* hearing it, but in the end he agreed to go out and ask Klaus Detterick a couple of questions. Mostly, I think, so he could be sure I wouldn't. "He's only thirty-nine, but he looks like an old man these days," McGee said, "and he don't need a smartass prison guard who thinks he's a detective to stir him up just when some of the sorrow has started to settle. You stay right here in town. I don't want you within hailing distance of the Detterick farm, but I want to be able to find you when I'm done talking to Klaus. If you start feeling restless, have a piece of pie down there in the diner. It'll weight you down." I ended up having two pieces, and it *was* kind of heavy.

When McGee came into the diner and sat down at the counter next to me, I tried to read his face and failed. "Well?" I asked.

"Come on home with me, we'll talk there," he said. "This place is a mite too public for my taste."

We had our conference on Rob McGee's front porch. Both of us were bundled up and chilly, but Mrs. McGee didn't allow smoking anywhere in her house. She was a woman ahead of her time. McGee talked awhile. He did it like a man who doesn't in the least enjoy what he's hearing out of his own mouth.

"It proves nothing, you know that, don't you?" he

asked when he was pretty well done. His tone was belligerent, and he poked his home-rolled cigarette at me in an aggressive way as he spoke, but his face was sick. Not all proof is what you see and hear in a court of law, and we both knew it. I have an idea that was the only time in his life when Deputy McGee wished he was as country-dumb as his boss.

"I know," I said.

"And if you're thinking of getting him a new trial on the basis of this one thing, you better think again, señor. John Coffey is a Negro, and in Trapingus County we're awful particular about giving new trials to Negroes."

"I know that, too."

"So what are you going to do?"

I pitched my cigarette over the porch rail and into the street. Then I stood up. It was going to be a long, cold ride back home, and the sooner I got going the sooner the trip would be done. "That I wish I did know, Deputy McGee," I said, "but I don't. The only thing I know tonight for a fact is that second piece of pie was a mistake."

"I'll tell you something, smart guy," he said, still speaking in that tone of hollow belligerence. "I don't think you should have opened Pandora's Box in the first place."

"It wasn't me opened it," I said, and then drove home.

I got there late—after midnight—but my wife was waiting up for me. I'd suspected she would be, but it still did my heart good to see her, and to have her put her arms around my neck and her body nice and firm against mine. "Hello, stranger," she said, and then touched me down below. "Nothing wrong with this fellow now, is there? He's just as healthy as can be."

"Yes, ma'am," I said, and lifted her up in my arms. I took her into the bedroom and we made love as sweet as sugar, and as I came to my climax, that delicious feeling of going out and letting go, I thought of John Coffey's endlessly weeping eyes. And of Melinda Moores saying *I dreamed you were wandering in the dark, and so was I.*

Still lying on top of my wife, with her arms around my neck and our thighs together, I began to weep myself.

"Paul!" she said, shocked and afraid. I don't think she'd seen me in tears more than half a dozen times before in the entire course of our marriage. I have never been, in the ordinary course of things, a crying man. "Paul, what is it?"

"I know everything there is to know," I said through my tears. "I know too goddam much, if you want to know the truth. I'm supposed to electrocute John Coffey in less than a week's time, but it was William Wharton who killed the Detterick girls. It was Wild Bill.''

5

The next day, the same bunch of screws who had eaten lunch in my kitchen after the botched Delacroix execution ate lunch there again. This time there was a fifth at our council of war: my wife. It was Jan who convinced me to tell the others; my first impulse had been not to. Wasn't it bad enough, I asked her, that *we* knew?

"You're not thinking clear about it," she'd answered. "Probably because you're still upset. They already know the worst thing, that John's on the spot for a crime he didn't commit. If anything, this makes it a little better."

I wasn't so sure, but I deferred to her judgement. I expected an uproar when I told Brutal, Dean, and Harry what I knew (I couldn't prove it, but I knew, all right), but at first there was only thoughtful silence. Then, taking another of Janice's biscuits and beginning to put an outrageous amount of butter on it, Dean said: "Did John see him, do you think? Did he see Wharton drop the girls, maybe even rape them?"

"I think if he'd seen that, he would have tried to stop it," I said. "As for seeing Wharton, maybe as he ran off, I suppose he might have. If he did, he forgot it later."

"Sure," Dean said. "He's special, but that doesn't make him bright. He only found out it was Wharton when Wharton reached through the bars of his cell and touched him."

Brutal was nodding. "That's why John looked so surprised ... so shocked. Remember the way his eyes opened?"

I nodded. "He used Percy on Wharton like a gun, that was what Janice said, and it was what I kept thinking about. Why would John Coffey want to kill Wild Bill? *Percy*, maybe—Percy stamped on Delacroix's mouse right in front of him, Percy burned Delacroix alive and John knew it—but Wharton? Wharton messed with most of us in one way or another, but he didn't mess with John at all, so far as I know—hardly passed four dozen words with him the whole time they were on the Mile together, and half of those were that last night. Why would he want to? He was from Purdom County, and as far as white boys from up there are concerned, you don't even see a Negro unless he happens to step into your road. So why did he do it? What could he've seen or felt when Wharton touched him that was so bad that he saved back the poison he took out of Melly's body?"

"And half-killed himself doing it, too," Brutal said.

"More like three-quarters. And the Detterick twins were all I could think of that was bad enough to explain what he did. I told myself the idea was nuts, too much of a coincidence, it just couldn't be. Then I remembered something Curtis Anderson wrote in the first memo I ever got about Wharton—that Wharton was crazy-wild, and that he'd rambled all over the state before the holdup where he killed all those people. *Rambled all over the state.* That stuck with me. Then there was the way he tried to choke Dean when he came in. That got me thinking about—"

"The dog," Dean said. He was rubbing his neck where Wharton had wrapped the chain. I don't think he even knew he was doing it. "How the dog's neck was broken."

"Anyway, I went on up to Purdom County to check Wharton's court records—all we had here were the reports on the murders that got him to the Green Mile. The end of his career, in other words. I wanted the beginning."

"Lot of trouble?" Brutal asked.

"Yeah. Vandalism, petty theft, setting haystack fires, even theft of an explosive—he and a friend swiped a stick of dynamite and set it off down by a creek. He got going early, ten years old, but what I wanted wasn't there. Then the Sheriff turned up to see who I was and what I was doing, and that was actually lucky. I fibbed, told him that a cell-search had turned up a bunch of pictures in Wharton's mattress—little girls with no clothes on. I said I'd wanted to see if Wharton had any kind of history as a pederast, because there were a couple of unsolved cases up in Tennessee that I'd heard about. I was careful never to mention the Detterick twins. I don't think they crossed his mind, either."

"Course not," Harry said. "Why would they have? That case is solved, after all."

"I said I guessed there was no sense chasing the idea, since there was nothing in Wharton's back file. I mean, there was *plenty* in the file, but none of it about that sort of thing. Then the Sheriff—Catlett, his name is—laughed and said not everything a bad apple like Bill Wharton did was in the court files, and what did it matter, anyway? He was dead, wasn't he?

"I said I was doing it just to satisfy my own curiosity, nothing else, and that relaxed him. He took me back to his office, sat me down, gave me a cup of coffee and a sinker, and told me that sixteen months ago, when Wharton was barely eighteen, a man in the western part of the county caught him in the barn with his daughter. It wasn't rape, exactly; the fellow described it to Catlett as 'not much more'n stink-finger.' Sorry, honey."

"That's all right," Janice said. She looked pale, though.

"How old was the girl?" Brutal asked.

"Nine," I said.

He winced.

"The man might've taken off after Wharton him-self, if he'd had him some big old brothers or cousins to give him a help, but he didn't. So he went to Catlett, but made it clear he only wanted Wharton warned. No one wants a nasty thing like that right out in public, if it can be helped. Anyway, Sheriff C. had been dealing with Wharton's antics for quite some time—had him in the reform school up that way for eight months or so when Wharton was fif-teen—and he decided enough was enough. He got three deputies, they went out to the Wharton place, set Missus Wharton aside when she started to weep and wail, and then they warned Mr. William 'Billy the Kid' Wharton what happens to big pimple-faced galoots who go up in the hayloft with girls not even old enough to have heard about their monthly courses, let alone started them. 'We warned that little punk good,' Catlett told me. 'Warned him until his head was bleedin, his shoulder was dislocated, and his ass was damn near broke.' "

Brutal was laughing in spite of himself. "That sounds like Purdom County, all right," he said. "Like as not."

"It was three months later, give or take, that Wharton broke out and started the spree that ended with the holdup," I said. "That and the murders that got him to us."

"So he'd had something to do with an underage girl once," Harry said. He took off his glasses, huffed on them, polished them. "*Way* underage. Once isn't exactly a pattern, is it?"

"A man doesn't do a thing like that just once," my wife said, then pressed her lips together so tight they almost weren't there.

Next I told them about my visit to Trapingus County. I'd been a lot more frank with Rob McGee— I'd had no choice, really. To this day I have no idea what sort of story he spun for Mr. Detterick, but the McGee who sat down next to me in the diner seemed to have aged seven years.

In mid-May, about a month before the holdup and the murders which finished Wharton's short career as an outlaw, Klaus Detterick had painted his barn (and, incidentally, Bowser's doghouse next to it). He hadn't wanted his son crawling around up on a high scaffolding, and the boy had been in school, anyway, so he had hired a fellow. A nice enough fellow. Very quiet. Three days' work it had been. No, the fellow hadn't slept at the house, Detterick wasn't foolish enough to believe that nice and quiet always meant safe, especially in those days, when there was so much dust-bowl riffraff on the roads. A man with a family had to be careful. In any case, the man hadn't needed lodging; he told Detterick he had taken a room in town, at Eva Price's. There *was* a lady named Eva Price in Tefton, and she *did* rent rooms, but she hadn't had a boarder that May who fit the description of Detterick's hired man, just the usual fellows in checked suits and derby hats, hauling sample cases— drummers, in other words. McGee had been able to tell me that because he stopped at Mrs. Price's and checked on his way back from the Detterick farm— that's how upset he was.

"Even so," he added, "there's no law against a man sleeping rough in the woods, Mr. Edgecombe. I've done it a time or two myself."

The hired man didn't sleep at the Dettericks' house, but he took dinner with them twice. He would have met Howie. He would have met the girls, Cora and Kathe. He would have listened to their chatter, some of which might have been about how much they looked forward to the coming summer, because if they were good and the weather was good, Mommy sometimes let them sleep out on the porch, where they could pretend they were pioneer wives crossing the Great Plains in Conestoga wagons.

I can see him sitting there at the table, eating roast chicken and Mrs. Detterick's rye bread, listening, keeping his wolf's eyes well veiled, nodding, smiling a little, storing it all up.

"This doesn't sound like the wildman you told me about when he first came on the Mile, Paul," Janice said doubtfully. "Not a bit."

"You didn't see him up at Indianola Hospital, ma'am," Harry said. "Just standin there with his mouth open and his bare butt hangin out the back of his johnny. Lettin us dress him. We thought he was either drugged or foolish. Didn't we, Dean?"

Dean nodded.

"The day after he finished the barn and left, a man wearing a bandanna mask robbed Hampey's Freight Office in Jarvis," I told them. "Got away with seventy dollars. He also took an 1892 silver dollar the freight agent carried as a lucky piece. That silver dollar was on Wharton when he was captured, and Jarvis is only thirty miles from Tefton."

"So this robber . . . this wildman . . . you think he

stopped for three days to help Klaus Detterick paint his barn," my wife said. "Ate dinner with them and said please pass the peas just like folks."

"The scariest thing about men like him is how unpredictable they are," Brutal said. "He might've been planning to kill the Dettericks and rifle their house, then changed his mind because a cloud came over the sun at the wrong time, or something like. Maybe he just wanted to cool off a little. But most likely he already had his eye on those two girls and was planning to come back. Do you think, Paul?"

I nodded. Of course I thought it. "And then there's the name he gave Detterick."

"What name?" Jan asked.

"Will Bonney."

"Bonney? I don't—"

"It was Billy the Kid's real name."

"Oh." Then her eyes widened. "Oh! So you *can* get John Coffey off! Thank God! All you have to do is show Mr. Detterick a picture of William Wharton ... his mug-shot should do ..."

Brutal and I exchanged an uncomfortable look. Dean was looking a bit hopeful, but Harry was staring down at his hands, as if all at once fabulously interested in his fingernails.

"What's wrong?" Janice asked. "Why are you

looking at each other that way? Surely this man McGee will have to—"

"Rob McGee struck me as a good man, and I think he's a hell of a law officer," I said, "but he swings no weight in Trapingus County. The power there is Sheriff Cribus, and the day he reopens the Detterick case on the basis of what I was able to find out would be the day it snows in hell."

"But . . . if Wharton was there . . . if Detterick can identify a picture of him and they *know* he was there . . ."

"Him being there in May doesn't mean he came back and killed those girls in June," Brutal said. He spoke in a low, gentle voice, the way you speak when you're telling someone there's been a death in the family. "On one hand you've got this fellow who helped Klaus Detterick paint a barn and then went away. Turns out he was committing crimes all over the place, but there's nothing against him for the three days in May he was around Tefton. On the other hand, you've got this big Negro, this *huge* Negro, that you found on the riverbank, holding two little dead girls, both of them naked, in his arms."

He shook his head.

"Paul's right, Jan. McGee may have his doubts, but McGee doesn't matter. Cribus is the only one who can reopen the case, and Cribus doesn't want to mess with what he thinks of as a happy ending—'it was a nigger,' thinks he, 'and not one of our'n in any case. Beautiful. I'll go up there to Cold Mountain, have me a steak and a draft beer at Ma's, then watch him fry, and there's an end to it.' "

Janice listened to all this with a mounting expression of horror on her face, then turned to me. "But McGee believes it, doesn't he, Paul? I could see it on your face. Deputy McGee knows he arrested the wrong man. Won't he stand up to the Sheriff?"

"All he can do by standing up to him is lose his job," I said. "Yes, I think that in his heart he knows it was Wharton. But what he says to himself is that, if he keeps his mouth shut and plays the game until Cribus either retires or eats himself to death, he gets the job. And things will be different then. That's what he tells himself to get to sleep, I imagine. And he's probably not so much different than Homer about one thing. He'll tell himself, 'After all, it's only a Negro. It's not like they're going to burn a white man for it.' "

"Then you'll have to go to them," Janice said, and my heart turned cold at the decisive, no-doubt-about-it tone of her voice. "Go and tell them what you found out."

"And how should we tell them we found it out, Jan?" Brutal asked her in that same low voice.

"Should we tell them about how Wharton grabbed John while we were taking him out of the prison to work a miracle on the Warden's wife?"

"No . . . of course not, but . . ." She saw how thin the ice was in that direction and skated in another one. "Lie, then," she said. She looked defiantly at Brutal, then turned that look on me. It was hot enough to smoke a hole in newspaper, you'd have said.

"Lie," I repeated. "Lie about what?"

"About what got you going, first up to Purdom County and then down to Trapingus. Go down there to that fat old Sheriff Cribus and say that Wharton *told* you he raped and murdered the Detterick girls. That he confessed." She switched her hot gaze to Brutal for a moment. "You can back him up, Brutus. You can say you were there when he confessed, you heard it, too. Why, Percy probably heard it as well, and that was probably what set him off. He shot Wharton because he couldn't stand thinking of what Wharton had done to those children. It snapped his mind. Just . . . What? What *now*, in the name of God?"

It wasn't just me and Brutal; Harry and Dean were looking at her, too, with a kind of horror.

"We never *reported* anything like that, ma'am," Harry said. He spoke as if talking to a child. "The first thing people'd ask is why we didn't. We're supposed to report anything our cell-babies say about prior crimes. Theirs or anyone else's."

"Not that we would've believed him," Brutal put in. "A man like Wild Bill Wharton lies about anything, Jan. Crimes he's committed, bigshots he's known, women he's gone to bed with, touchdowns he scored in high school, even the damn weather."

"But . . . but . . ." Her face was agonized. I went to put my arm around her and she pushed it violently away. *"But he was there! He painted their goddamned barn! HE ATE DINNER WITH THEM!"*

"All the more reason why he might take credit for the crime," Brutal said. "After all, what harm? Why not boast? You can't fry a man twice, after all."

"Let me see if I've got this right. We here at this table know that not only did John Coffey not kill those girls, he was trying to save their lives. Deputy McGee doesn't know all that, of course, but he *does* have a pretty good idea that the man condemned to die for the murders didn't do them. And still . . . *still* . . . you can't get him a new trial. Can't even reopen the case."

"Yessum," Dean said. He was polishing his glasses furiously. "That's about the size of it."

She sat with her head lowered, thinking. Brutal started to say something and I raised a hand, shushing him. I didn't believe Janice could think of a way to get John out of the killing box he was in, but I didn't believe it was impossible, either. She was a fearsomely smart lady, my wife. Fearsomely determined, as well. That's a combination that sometimes turns mountains into valleys.

"All right," she said at last. "Then you've got to get him out on your own."

"Ma'am?" Harry looked flabbergasted. Frightened, too.

"You can do it. You did it once, didn't you? You can do it again. Only this time you won't bring him back."

"Would you want to be the one to explain to my kids why their daddy is in prison, Missus Edgecombe?" Dean asked. "Charged with helping a murderer escape jail?"

"There won't be any of that, Dean; we'll work out a plan. Make it look like a real escape."

"Make sure it's a plan that could be worked out by a fellow who can't even remember how to tie his own shoes, then," Harry said. "They'll have to believe that."

She looked at him uncertainly.

"It wouldn't do any good," Brutal said. "Even if we could think of a way, it wouldn't do any good."

"Why not?" She sounded as if she might be going to cry. "Just why the damn hell not?"

"Because he's a six-foot-eight-inch baldheaded black man with barely enough brains to feed himself," I said. "How long do you think it would be before he was recaptured? Two hours? Six?"

"He got along without attracting much attention before," she said. A tear trickled down her cheek. She slapped it away with the heel of her hand.

That much was true. I had written letters to some friends and relatives of mine farther down south, asking if they'd seen anything in the papers about a man fitting John Coffey's description. Anything at all. Janice had done the same. We had come up with just one possible sighting so far, in the town of Muscle Shoals, Alabama. A twister had struck a church there during choir practice—in 1929, this had been—and a large black man had hauled two fellows out of the rubble. Both had looked dead to onlookers at first, but as it turned out, neither had been even seriously hurt. It was like a miracle, one of the witnesses was quoted as saying. The black man, a drifter who had been hired by the church pastor to do a day's worth of chores, had disappeared in the excitement.

"You're right, he got along," Brutal said. "But you have to remember that he did most of his getting along before he was convicted of raping and murdering two little girls."

She sat without answering. She sat that way for almost a full minute, and then she did something which shocked me as badly as my sudden flow of tears must have shocked her. She reached out and shoved everything off the table with one wide sweep of her arm—plates, glasses, cups, silverware, the bowl of collards, the bowl of squash, the platter with the carved ham on it, the milk, the pitcher of cold tea. All off the table and onto the floor, ker-smash.

"Holy shit!" Dean cried, rocking back from the table so hard he damned near went over on his back.

Janice ignored him. It was Brutal and me she was looking at, mostly me. "Do you mean to kill him, you cowards?" she asked. "Do you mean to kill the man who saved Melinda Moores's life, who tried to save those little girls' lives? Well, at least there will be one less black man in the world, won't there? You can console yourselves with that. *One less nigger.*"

She got up, looked at her chair, and kicked it into the wall. It rebounded and fell into the spilled squash. I took her wrist and she yanked it free.

"Don't touch me," she said. "Next week this time you'll be a murderer, no better than that man Wharton, so don't touch me."

She went out onto the back stoop, put her apron

up to her face, and began to sob into it. The four of us looked at each other. After a little bit I got on my feet and set about cleaning up the mess. Brutal joined me first, then Harry and Dean. When the place looked more or less shipshape again, they left. None of us said a word the whole time. There was really nothing left to say.

6

That was my night off. I sat in the living room of our little house, smoking cigarettes, listening to the radio, and watching the dark come up out of the ground to swallow the sky. Television is all right, I've nothing against it, but I don't like how it turns you away from the rest of the world and toward nothing but its own glassy self. In that one way, at least, radio was better.

Janice came in, knelt beside the arm of my chair, and took my hand. For a little while neither of us said anything, just stayed that way, listening to *Kay Kyser's Kollege of Musical Knowledge* and watching the stars come out. It was all right with me.

"I'm so sorry I called you a coward," she said. "I feel worse about that than anything I've ever said to you in our whole marriage."

"Even the time when we went camping and you

called me Old Stinky Sam?" I asked, and then we laughed and had a kiss or two and it was better again between us. She was so beautiful, my Janice, and I still dream of her. Old and tired of living as I am, I'll dream that she walks into my room in this lonely, forgotten place where the hallways all smell of piss and old boiled cabbage, I dream she's young and beautiful with her blue eyes and her fine high breasts that I couldn't hardly keep my hands off of, and she'll say, *Why, honey, I wasn't in that bus crash. You made a mistake, that's all.* Even now I dream that, and sometimes when I wake up and know it was a dream, I cry. I, who hardly ever cried at all when I was young.

"Does Hal know?" she asked at last.

"That John's innocent? I don't see how he can."

"Can he help? Does he have any influence with Cribus?"

"Not a bit, honey."

She nodded, as if she had expected this. "Then don't tell him. If he can't help, for God's sake don't tell him."

"No."

She looked up at me with steady eyes. "And you won't call in sick that night. None of you will. You can't."

"No, we can't. If we're there, we can at least make

it quick for him. We can do that much. It won't be like Delacroix." For a moment, mercifully brief, I saw the black silk mask burning away from Del's face and revealing the cooked blobs of jelly which had been his eyes.

"There's no way out for you, is there?" She took my hand, rubbed it down the soft velvet of her cheek. "Poor Paul. Poor old guy."

I said nothing. Never before or after in my life did I feel so much like running from a thing. Just taking Jan with me, the two of us with a single packed carpetbag between us, running to anywhere.

"My poor old guy," she repeated, and then: "Talk to him."

"Who? John?"

"Yes. Talk to him. Find out what *he* wants."

I thought about it, then nodded. She was right. She usually was.

7

Two days later, on the eighteenth, Bill Dodge, Hank Bitterman, and someone else—I don't remember who, some floater—took John Coffey over to D Block for his shower, and we rehearsed his execution while he was gone. We didn't let Toot-Toot stand in for John; all of us knew, even without talking about it, that it would have been an obscenity.

I did it.

"John Coffey," Brutal said in a not-quite-steady voice as I sat clamped into Old Sparky, "you have been condemned to die in the electric chair, sentence passed by a jury of your peers ..."

John Coffey's peers? What a joke. So far as I knew, there was no one like him on the planet. Then I thought of what John had said while he stood looking at Sparky from the foot of the stairs leading down from my office: *They're still in there. I hear them screaming.*

"Get me out of it," I said hoarsely. "Undo these clamps and let me up."

They did it, but for a moment I felt frozen there, as if Old Sparky did not want to let me go.

As we walked back to the block, Brutal spoke to me in a low voice, so not even Dean and Harry, who were setting up the last of the chairs behind us, would overhear. "I done a few things in my life that I'm not proud of, but this is the first time I ever felt really actually in danger of hell."

I looked at him to make sure he wasn't joking. I didn't think he was. "What do you mean?"

"I mean we're fixing to kill a gift of God," he said. "One that never did ary harm to us, or to anyone else. What am I going to say if I end up standing in front of God the Father Almighty and He asks me to explain why I did it? That it was my job? My *job*?"

8

When John got back from his shower and the floaters had left, I unlocked his cell, went in, and sat down on the bunk beside him. Brutal was on the desk. He looked up, saw me in there on my own, but said nothing. He just went back to whatever paperwork he was currently mangling, licking away at the tip of his pencil the whole time.

John looked at me with his strange eyes—bloodshot, distant, on the verge of tears . . . and yet calm, too, as if crying was not such a bad way of life, not once you got used to it. He even smiled a little. He smelled of Ivory soap, I remember, as clean and fresh as a baby after his evening bath.

"Hello, boss," he said, and then reached out and took both of my hands in both of his. It was done with a perfect unstudied naturalness.

"Hello, John." There was a little block in my

throat, and I tried to swallow it away. "I guess you know that we're coming down to it now. Another couple of days."

He said nothing, only sat there holding my hands in his. I think, looking back on it, that something had already begun to happen to me, but I was too fixed—mentally and emotionally—on doing my duty to notice.

"Is there anything special you'd like that night for dinner, John? We can rustle you up most anything. Even bring you a beer, if you want. Just have to put her in a coffee cup, that's all."

"Never got the taste," he said.

"Something special to eat, then?"

His brow creased below that expanse of clean brown skull. Then the lines smoothed out and he smiled. "Meatloaf'd be good."

"Meatloaf it is. With gravy and mashed." I felt a tingle like you get in your arm when you've slept on it, except this one was all over my body. *In* my body. "What else to go with it?"

"Dunno, boss. Whatever you got, I guess. Okra, maybe, but I's not picky."

"All right," I said, and thought he would also have Mrs. Janice Edgecombe's peach cobbler for dessert. "Now, what about a preacher? Someone you could say a little prayer with, night after next? It comforts a man, I've seen that many times. I could get in touch with Reverend Schuster, he's the man who came when Del—"

"Don't want no preacher," John said. "You been good to me, boss. You can say a prayer, if you want. That'd be all right. I could get kneebound with you a bit, I guess."

"*Me!* John, I couldn't—"

He pressed down on my hands a little, and that feeling got stronger. "You *could*," he said. "Couldn't you, boss?"

"I suppose so," I heard myself say. My voice seemed to have developed an echo. "I suppose I could, if it came to that."

The feeling was strong inside me by then, and it was like before, when he'd cured my waterworks, but it was different, too. And not just because there was nothing wrong with me this time. It was different because *this time he didn't know he was doing it*. Suddenly I was terrified, almost choked with a need to get out of there. Lights were going on inside me where there had never been lights before. Not just in my brain; all over my body.

"You and Mr. Howell and the other bosses been good to me," John Coffey said. "I know you been worryin, but you ought to quit on it now. Because I *want* to go, boss."

I tried to speak and couldn't. He could, though. What he said next was the longest I ever heard him speak.

"I'm rightly tired of the pain I hear and feel, boss. I'm tired of bein on the road, lonely as a robin in the rain. Not never havin no buddy to go on with or tell me where we's comin from or goin to or why. I'm tired of people bein ugly to each other. It feels like pieces of glass in my head. I'm tired of all the times I've wanted to help and couldn't. I'm tired of bein in the dark. Mostly it's the pain. There's too much. If I could end it, I would. But I cain't."

Stop it, I tried to say. Stop it, let go of my hands, I'm going to drown if you don't. Drown or explode.

"You won't 'splode," he said, smiling a little at the idea . . . but he let go of my hands.

I leaned forward, gasping. Between my knees I could see every crack in the cement floor, every groove, every flash of mica. I looked up at the wall and saw names that had been written there in 1924, 1926, 1931. Those names had been washed away, the men who had written them had also been washed away, in a manner of speaking, but I guess you can never wash anything completely away, not from this dark glass of a world, and now I saw them again, a tangle of names overlying one another, and looking at them was like listening to the dead speak and sing and cry out for mercy. I felt my eyeballs pulsing in their sockets, heard my own heart, felt the windy whoosh of my blood rushing through all the boulevards of my body like letters being mailed to everywhere.

I heard a train-whistle in the distance—the three-fifty to Priceford, I imagine, but I couldn't be sure, because I'd never heard it before. Not from Cold Mountain, I hadn't, because the closest it came to the state pen was ten miles east. I *couldn't* have heard it from the pen, so you would have said and so, until November of '32, I would have believed, but I heard it that day.

Somewhere a lightbulb shattered, loud as a bomb.

"What did you do to me?" I whispered. "Oh John, what did you do?"

"I'm sorry, boss," he said in his calm way. "I wasn't thinkin. Ain't much, I reckon. You feel like regular soon."

I got up and went to the cell door. It felt like walking in a dream. When I got there, he said: "You wonder why they didn't scream. That's the only thing you still wonder about, ain't it? Why those two little girls didn't scream while they were still there on the porch."

I turned and looked at him. I could see every red snap in his eyes, I could see every pore on his face

. . . and I could feel his hurt, the pain that he took in from other people like a sponge takes in water. I could see the darkness he had spoken of, too. It lay in all the spaces of the world as he saw it, and in that moment I felt both pity for him and great relief. Yes, it was a terrible thing we'd be doing, nothing would ever change that . . . and yet we would be doing him a favor.

"I seen it when that bad fella, he done grab me," John said. "That's when I knowed it was him done it. I seen him that day, I was in the trees and I seen him drop them down and run away, but—"

"You forgot," I said.

"That's right, boss. Until he touch me, I forgot."

"Why *didn't* they scream, John? He hurt them enough to make them bleed, their parents were right upstairs, so why didn't they scream?"

John looked at me from his haunted eyes. "He say to the one, 'If you make noise, it's your sister I kill, not you.' He say that same to the other. You see?"

"Yes," I whispered, and I *could* see it. The Detterick porch in the dark. Wharton leaning over them like a ghoul. One of them had maybe started to cry out, so Wharton had hit her and she had bled from the nose. That's where most of it had come from.

"He kill them with they love," John said. "They love for each other. You see how it was?"

I nodded, incapable of speech.

He smiled. The tears were flowing again, but he smiled. "That's how it is every day," he said, "all over the worl'." Then he lay down and turned his face to the wall.

I stepped out into the Mile, locked his cell, and walked up to the duty desk. I still felt like a man in a dream. I realized I could hear Brutal's thoughts— a very faint whisper, how to spell some word, *receive*, I think it was. He was thinking i *before* e, *except after* c, *is that how the dadratted thing goes?* Then he looked up, started to smile, and stopped when he got a good look at me. "Paul?" he asked. "Are you all right?"

"Yes." Then I told him what John had told me— not all of it, and certainly not about what his touch had done to me (I never told anyone that part, not even Janice; Elaine Connelly will be the first to know of it—if, that is, she wants to read these last pages after reading all the rest of them), but I repeated what John had said about wanting to go. That seemed to relieve Brutal—a bit, anyway—but I sensed (heard?) him wondering if I hadn't made it up, just to set his mind at ease. Then I felt him deciding to believe it, simply because it would make things a little easier for him when the time came.

"Paul, is that infection of yours coming back?" he asked. "You look all flushed."

"No, I think I'm okay," I said. I wasn't, but I felt sure by then that John was right and I was going to be. I could feel that tingle starting to subside.

"All the same, it might not hurt you to go on in your office there and lie down a bit."

Lying down was the *last* thing I felt like right then—the idea seemed so ridiculous that I almost laughed. What I felt like doing was maybe building myself a little house, then shingling it, and plowing a garden in back, and planting it. All before suppertime.

That's how it is, I thought. *Every day. All over the world. That darkness. All over the world.*

"I'm going to take a turn over to Admin instead. Got a few things to check over there."

"If you say so."

I went to the door and opened it, then looked back. "You've got it right," I said: "r-e-c-e-i-v-e; *i* before *e*, except after *c*. Most of the time, anyway; I guess there's exceptions to all the rules."

I went out, not needing to look back at him to know he was staring with his mouth open.

I kept moving for the rest of that shift, unable to sit down for more than five minutes at a stretch before jumping up again. I went over to Admin, and then I tromped back and forth across the empty exercise yard until the guards in the towers must have thought I was crazy. But by the time my shift was over, I was starting to calm down again, and that rustle of thoughts in my head—like a stirring of leaves, it was—had pretty much quieted down.

Still, halfway home that morning, it came back strong. The way my urinary infection had. I had to park my Ford by the side of the road, get out, and sprint nearly half a mile, head down, arms pumping, breath tearing in and out of my throat as warm as something that you've carried in your armpit. Then, at last, I began to feel really normal. I trotted halfway back to where the Ford was parked and walked the rest of the way, my breath steaming in the chilly air. When I got home, I told Janice that John Coffey had said he was ready, that he wanted to go. She nodded, looking relieved. Was she really? I couldn't say. Six hours before, even three, I would have known, but by then I didn't. And that was good. John had kept saying that he was tired, and now I could understand why. It would have tired anyone out, what he had. Would have made anyone long for rest and for quiet.

When Janice asked me why I looked so flushed and smelled so sweaty, I told her I had stopped the car on my way home and gone running for awhile, running hard. I told her that much—as I may have said (there's too many pages here now for me to want to look back through and make sure), lying wasn't much a part of our marriage—but I didn't tell her why.

And she didn't ask.

9

There were no thunderstorms on the night it came John Coffey's turn to walk the Green Mile. It was seasonally cold for those parts at that time of year, in the thirties, I'd guess, and a million stars spilled across used-up, picked-out fields where frost glittered on fenceposts and glowed like diamonds on the dry skeletons of July's corn.

Brutus Howell was out front for this one—he would do the capping and tell Van Hay to roll when it was time. Bill Dodge was in with Van Hay. And, at around eleven-twenty on the night of November 20th, Dean and Harry and I went down to our one occupied cell, where John Coffey sat on the end of his bunk with his hands clasped between his knees and a tiny dab of meatloaf gravy on the collar of his blue shirt. He looked out through the bars at us, a lot calmer than we felt, it seemed. My hands were cold and my temples were throbbing. It was one thing to know he was willing—it made it at least possible for us to do our job—but it was another to know we were going to electrocute him for someone else's crime.

I had last seen Hal Moores around seven that evening. He was in his office, buttoning up his overcoat. His face was pale, his hands shaking so badly that he was making quite some production of those buttons. I almost wanted to knock his fingers aside and do the coat up myself, like you would with a little kid. The irony was that Melinda had looked better when Jan and I went to see her the previous weekend than Hal had looked earlier on John Coffey's execution evening.

"I won't be staying for this one," he had said. "Curtis will be there, and I know Coffey will be in good hands with you and Brutus."

"Yes, sir, we'll do our best," I said. "Is there any word on Percy?" Is he coming back around? is what I meant, of course. Is he even now sitting in a room somewhere and telling someone—some doctor, most likely—about how we zipped him into the nut-coat and threw him into the restraint room like any other problem child ... any other lugoon, in Percy's language? And if he is, are they believing him?

6. COFFEY ON THE MILE

But according to Hal, Percy was just the same. Not talking, and not, so far as anyone could tell, in the world at all. He was still at Indianola—"being evaluated," Hal had said, looking mystified at the phrase—but if there was no improvement, he would be moving along soon.

"How's Coffey holding up?" Hal had asked then. He had finally managed to do up the last button of his coat.

I nodded. "He'll be fine, Warden."

He'd nodded back, then gone to the door, looking old and ill. "How can so much good and so much evil live together in the same man? How could the man who cured my wife be the same man who killed those little girls? Do you understand that?"

I had told him I didn't, the ways of God were mysterious, there was good and evil in all of us, ours not to reason why, hotcha, hotcha, row-dee-dow. Most of what I told him were things I'd learned in the church of Praise Jesus, The Lord Is Mighty, Hal nodding the whole time and looking sort of exalted. He could afford to nod, couldn't he? Yes. And look exalted, too. There was a deep sadness on his face— he was shaken, all right; I never doubted it—but there were no tears this time, because he had a wife to go home to, his companion to go home to, and she was fine. Thanks to John Coffey, she was well and fine and the man who had signed John's death warrant could leave and go to her. He didn't have to watch what came next. He would be able to sleep that night in his wife's warmth while John Coffey lay on a slab in the basement of County Hospital, growing cool as the friendless, speechless hours moved toward dawn. And I hated Hal for those things. Just a little, and I'd get over it, but it was hate, all right. The genuine article.

Now I stepped into the cell, followed by Dean and Harry, both of them pale and downcast. "Are you ready, John?" I asked.

He nodded. "Yes, boss. Guess so."

"All right, then. I got a piece to say before we go out."

"You say what you need to, boss."

"John Coffey, as an officer of the court . . ."

I said it right to the end, and when I'd finished, Harry Terwilliger stepped up beside me and held out his hand. John looked surprised for a moment, then smiled and shook it. Dean, looking paler than ever, offered his next. "You deserve better than this, Johnny," he said hoarsely. "I'm sorry."

"I be all right," John said. "This the hard part; I be all right in a little while." He got up, and the St.

Christopher's medal Melly had given him swung free of his shirt.

"John, I ought to have that," I said. "I can put it back on you after the ... after, if you want, but I should take it for now." It was silver, and if it was lying against his skin when Jack Van Hay switched on the juice, it might fuse itself into his skin. Even if it didn't do that, it was apt to electroplate, leaving a kind of charred photograph of itself on the skin of his chest. I had seen it before. I'd seen most everything during my years on the Mile. More than was good for me. I knew that now.

He slipped the chain over his head and put it in my hand. I put the medallion in my pocket and told him to step on out of the cell. There was no need to check his head and make sure the contact would be firm and the induction good; it was as smooth as the palm of my hand.

"You know, I fell asleep this afternoon and had a dream, boss," he said. "I dreamed about Del's mouse."

"Did you, John?" I flanked him on the left. Harry took the right. Dean fell in behind, and then we were walking the Green Mile. For me, it was the last time I ever walked it with a prisoner.

"Yep," he said. "I dreamed he got down to that place Boss Howell talked about, that Mouseville place. I dreamed there was kids, and how they laughed at his tricks! My!" He laughed himself at the thought of it, then grew serious again. "I dreamed those two little blond-headed girls were there. They 'us laughin, too. I put my arms around em and there 'us no blood comin out they hair and they 'us fine. We all watch Mr. Jingles roll that spool, and how we did laugh. Fit to bus', we was."

"Is that so?" I was thinking I couldn't go through with it, just could not, there was no way. I was going to cry or scream or maybe my heart would burst with sorrow and that would be an end to it.

We went into my office. John looked around for a moment or two, then dropped to his knees without having to be asked. Behind him, Harry was looking at me with haunted eyes. Dean was as white as paper.

I got down on my knees with John and thought there was a funny turnaround brewing here: after all the prisoners I'd had to help up so they could finish the journey, this time I was the one who was apt to need a hand. That's the way it felt, anyway.

"What should we pray for, boss?" John asked.

"Strength," I said without even thinking. I closed my eyes and said, "Lord God of Hosts, please help us finish what we've started, and please welcome this man, John Coffey—like the drink but not spelled the same—into heaven and give him peace. Please help us to see him off the way he deserves and let nothing go wrong. Amen." I opened my eyes and looked at Dean and Harry. Both of them looked a little better. Probably it was having a few moments to catch their breath. I doubt it was my praying.

I started to get up, and John caught my arm. He gave me a look that was both timid and hopeful. "I 'member a prayer someone taught me when I 'us little," he said. "At least I think I do. Can I say it?"

"You go right on and do her," Dean said. "Lots of time yet, John."

John closed his eyes and frowned with concentration. I expected now-I-lay-me-down-to-sleep, or maybe a garbled version of the Lord's prayer, but I got neither; I had never heard what he came out with before, and have never heard it again, not that either the sentiments or expressions were particularly unusual. Holding his hands up in front of his closed eyes, John Coffey said: "Baby Jesus, meek and mild, pray for me, an orphan child. Be my strength, be my friend, be with me until the end. Amen." He opened his eyes, started to get up, then looked at me closely.

I wiped my arm across my eyes. As I listened to him, I had been thinking about Del; he had wanted to pray one more at the end, too. *Holy Mary, mother of God, pray for us sinners now, and at the hour of our death.* "Sorry, John."

"Don't be," he said. He squeezed my arm and smiled. And then, as I'd thought he might have to do, he helped me to my feet.

10

There weren't many witnesses—maybe fourteen in all, half the number that had been in the storage room for the Delacroix execution. Homer Cribus was there, overflowing his chair as per usual, but I didn't see Deputy McGee. Like Warden Moores, he had apparently decided to give this one a miss.

Sitting in the front row was an elderly couple I didn't recognize at first, even though I had seen their pictures in a good many newspaper articles by that day in the third week of November. Then, as we neared the platform where Old Sparky waited, the woman spat, "Die slow, you son of a bitch!" and I realized they were the Dettericks, Klaus and Marjorie. I hadn't recognized them because you don't often see elderly people who haven't yet climbed out of their thirties.

John hunched his shoulders at the sound of the

woman's voice and Sheriff Cribus's grunt of approval. Hank Bitterman, who had the guard-post near the front of the meager group of spectators, never took his eyes off Klaus Detterick. That was per my orders, but Detterick never made a move in John's direction that night. Detterick seemed to be on some other planet.

Brutal, standing beside Old Sparky, gave me a small finger-tilt as we stepped up onto the platform. He holstered his sidearm and took John's wrist, escorting him toward the electric chair as gently as a boy leading his date out onto the floor for their first dance as a couple.

"Everything all right, John?" he asked in a low voice.

"Yes, boss, but . . ." His eyes were moving from side to side in their sockets, and for the first time he looked and sounded scared. "But they's a lot of folks here hate me. A *lot*. I can feel it. Hurts. Bores in like bee-stings an' *hurts*."

"Feel how we feel, then," Brutal said in that same low voice. "*We* don't hate you—can you feel that?"

"Yes, boss." But his voice was trembling worse now, and his eyes had begun to leak their slow tears again.

"*Kill him twice, you boys!*" Marjorie Detterick suddenly screamed. Her ragged, strident voice was like a slap. John cringed against me and moaned. "*You go on and kill that raping baby-killer twice, that'd be just fine!*"

Klaus, still looking like a man dreaming awake, pulled her against his shoulder. She began to sob.

I saw with dismay that Harry Terwilliger was crying, too. So far none of the spectators had seen his tears—his back was to them—but he was crying, all right. Still, what could we do? Besides push on with it, I mean?

Brutal and I turned John around. Brutal pressed on one of the big man's shoulders and John sat. He gripped Sparky's wide oak arms, his eyes moving from side to side, his tongue darting out to wet first one corner of his mouth, then the other.

Harry and I dropped to our knees. The day before, we'd had one of the shop-trusties weld temporary flexible extensions to the chair's ankle clamps, because John Coffey's ankles were nigh on the size of an ordinary fellow's calves. Still, I had a nightmarish moment when I thought they were still going to come up small, and we'd have to take him back to his cell while Sam Broderick, who was head of the shop guys in those days, was found and tinkered some more. I gave a final, extra-hard shove with the heels of my hands and the clamp on my side closed. John's leg jerked and he gasped. I had pinched him.

"Sorry, John," I murmured, and glanced at Harry. He had gotten his clamp fixed more easily (either the extension on his side was a little bigger or John's right calf was a little smaller), but he was looking at the result with a doubtful expression. I guessed I could understand why; the modified clamps had a *hungry* look, their jaws seeming to gape like the mouths of alligators.

"It'll be all right," I said, hoping that I sounded convincing . . . and that I was telling the truth. "Wipe your face, Harry."

He swabbed at it with his arm, wiping away tears from his cheeks and beads of sweat from his forehead. We turned. Homer Cribus, who had been talking too loudly to the man sitting next to him (the prosecutor, judging from the string tie and rusty black suit), fell silent. It was almost time.

Brutal had clamped one of John's wrists, Dean the other. Over Dean's shoulder I could see the doctor, unobtrusive as ever, standing against the wall with his black bag between his feet. Nowadays I guess they just about run such affairs, especially the ones with the IV drips, but back then you almost had to yank them forward if you wanted them. Maybe back then they had a clearer idea of what was right for a doctor to be doing, and what was a perversion of the special promise they make, the one where they swear first of all to do no harm.

Dean nodded to Brutal. Brutal turned his head, seemed to glance at the telephone that was never going to ring for the likes of John Coffey, and called "Roll on one!" to Jack Van Hay.

There was that hum, like an old fridge kicking on, and the lights burned a little brighter. Our shadows stood out a little sharper, black shapes that climbed the wall and seemed to hover around the shadow of the chair like vultures. John drew in a sharp breath. His knuckles were white.

"Does it hurt yet?" Mrs. Detterick shrieked brokenly from against her husband's shoulder. *"I hope it does! I hope it hurts like hell!"* Her husband squeezed her. One side of his nose was bleeding, I saw, a narrow trickle of red working its way down into his narrow-gauge mustache. When I opened the paper the following March and saw he'd died of a stroke, I was about the least surprised man on earth.

Brutal stepped into John's field of vision. He touched John's shoulder as he spoke. That was irregular, but of the witnesses, only Curtis Anderson knew it, and he did not seem to remark it. I thought he looked like a man who only wants to be done with his current job. Desperately wants to be done with it. He enlisted in the Army after Pearl Harbor, but never got overseas; he died at Fort Bragg, in a truck accident.

John, meanwhile, relaxed beneath Brutal's fingers. I don't think he understood much, if any, of what Brutal was telling him, but he took comfort from Brutal's hand on his shoulder. Brutal, who died of a heart attack about twenty-five years later (he was eating a fish sandwich and watching TV wrestling when it happened, his sister said), was a good man. My friend. Maybe the best of us. He had no trouble understanding how a man could simultaneously want to go and still be terrified of the trip.

"John Coffey, you have been condemned to die in the electric chair, sentence passed by a jury of your peers and imposed by a judge of good standing in this state. God save the people of this state. Do you have anything to say before sentence is carried out?"

John wet his lips again, then spoke clearly. Six words. "I'm sorry for what I am."

"You ought to be!" the mother of the two dead girls screamed. *"Oh you monster, you ought to be! YOU DAMN WELL OUGHT TO BE!"*

John's eyes turned to me. I saw no resignation in them, no hope of heaven, no dawning peace. How I would love to tell you that I did. How I would love to tell myself that. What I saw was fear, misery, incompletion, and incomprehension. They were the eyes of a trapped and terrified animal. I thought of what he'd said about how Wharton had gotten Cora and Kathe Detterick off the porch without rousing the house: *He kill them with they love. That's how it is every day. All over the worl'.*

Brutal took the new mask from its brass hook on the back of the chair, but as soon as John saw it and understood what it was, his eyes widened in horror. He looked at me, and now I could see huge droplets of sweat standing out on the curve of his naked skull. As big as robin's eggs, they looked.

"Please, boss, don't put that thing over my face," he said in a moaning little whisper. "Please don't put me in the dark, don't make me go into the dark, I's afraid of the dark."

Brutal was looking at me, eyebrows raised, frozen in place, the mask in his hands. His eyes said it was my call, he'd go either way. I thought as fast as I could and as well as I could—hard to do, with my head pounding the way it was. The mask was tradition, not law. It was, in fact, to spare the witnesses. And suddenly I decided that they did not need to be spared, not this once. John, after all, hadn't done a damned thing in his life to warrant dying under a mask. They didn't know that, but we did, and I decided I was going to grant this last request. As for Marjorie Detterick, she'd probably send me a thank-you note.

"All right, John," I murmured.

Brutal put the mask back. From behind us, Homer Cribus called out indignantly in his deep-dish cracker voice: "Say, boy! Put that-air mask on him! Think we want to watch his eyes pop?"

"Be quiet, sir," I said without turning. "This is an execution, and you're not in charge of it."

"Any more than you were in charge of catching him, you tub of guts," Harry whispered. Harry died in 1982, close to the age of eighty. An old man. Not in my league, of course, but few are. It was intestinal cancer of some kind.

Brutal bent over and plucked the disk of sponge out of its bucket. He pressed a finger into it and licked the tip, but he hardly had to; I could see the ugly brown thing dripping. He tucked it into the cap, then put the cap on John's head. For the first time I saw that Brutal was pale, too—pasty white, on the verge of passing out. I thought of him saying that he felt, for the first time in his life, that he was in danger of hell, because we were fixing to kill a gift of God. I felt a sudden strong need to retch. I controlled it, but only with an effort. Water from the sponge was dripping down the sides of John's face.

Dean Stanton ran the strap—let out to its maximum length on this occasion—across John's chest and gave it to me. We had taken such pains to try and protect Dean on the night of our trip, because of his kids, never knowing that he had less than four months to live. After John Coffey, he requested and received a transfer away from Old Sparky, over to C Block, and there a prisoner stabbed him in the throat with a shank and let out his life's blood on the dirty board floor. I never knew why. I don't think anyone ever knew why. Old Sparky seems such a thing of perversity when I look back on those days, such a deadly bit of folly. Fragile as blown glass, we are, even under the best of conditions. To kill each other with gas and electricity, and in cold blood? The folly. The *horror.*

Brutal checked the strap, then stood back. I waited for him to speak, but he didn't. As he crossed his hands behind his back and stood at parade rest, I knew that he wouldn't. Perhaps couldn't. I didn't think I could, either, but then I looked at John's terrified, weeping eyes and knew I had to. Even if it damned me forever, I had to.

''Roll on two,'' I said in a dusty, cracking voice I hardly recognized as my own.

The cap hummed. Eight large fingers and two large thumbs rose from the ends of the chair's broad oak arms and splayed tensely in ten different directions, their tips jittering. His big knees made caged pistoning motions, but the clamps on his ankles held. Overhead, three of the hanging lights blew out—*Pow! Pow! Pow!* Marjorie Detterick screamed at the sound and fainted in her husband's arms. She died in Memphis, eighteen years later. Harry sent me the obit. It was a trolley-car accident.

John surged forward against the chest-strap. For a

moment his eyes met mine. They were aware; I was the last thing he saw as we tilted him off the edge of the world. Then he fell against the seatback, the cap coming askew on his head a little, smoke—a sort of charry mist—drifting out from beneath it. But on the whole, you know, it was quick. I doubt if it was painless, the way the chair's supporters always claim (it's not an idea even the most rabid of them ever seems to want to investigate personally), but it was quick. The hands were limp again, the formerly bluish-white moons at the base of the fingernails now a deep eggplant hue, a tendril of smoke rising off cheeks still wet with salt water from the sponge . . . and his tears.

John Coffey's last tears.

11

I was all right until I got home. It was dawn by then, and birds singing. I parked my flivver, I got out, I walked up the back steps, and then the second greatest grief I have ever known washed over me. It was thinking of how he'd been afraid of the dark that did it. I remembered the first time we'd met, how he'd asked if we left a light on at night, and my legs gave out on me. I sat on my steps and hung my head over my knees and cried. It didn't feel like that weeping was just for John, either, but for all of us.

Janice came out and sat down beside me. She put an arm over my shoulders.

"You didn't hurt him any more than you could help, did you?"

I shook my head no.

"And he wanted to go."

I nodded.

"Come in the house," she said, helping me up. It made me think of the way John had helped me up after we'd prayed together. "Come in and have coffee."

I did. The first morning passed, and the first afternoon, then the first shift back at work. Time takes it all, whether you want it to or not. Time takes it all, time bears it away, and in the end there is only darkness. Sometimes we find others in that darkness, and sometimes we lose them there again. That's all I know, except that this happened in 1932, when the state penitentiary was still at Cold Mountain.

And the electric chair, of course.

12

Around quarter past two in the afternoon, my friend Elaine Connelly came to me where I sat in the sunroom, with the last pages of my story squared up neatly in front of me. Her face was very pale, and there were shiny places under her eyes. I think she had been crying.

Me, I'd been looking. Just that. Looking out the window and over the hills to the east, my right hand throbbing at the end of its wrist. But it was a peaceful throb, somehow. I felt empty, husked out. A feeling that was terrible and wonderful at the same time.

It was hard to meet Elaine's eyes—I was afraid of the hate and contempt I might see there—but they were all right. Sad and wondering, but all right. No hate, no contempt, and no disbelief.

"Do you want the rest of the story?" I asked. I tapped the little pile of script with my aching hand.

"It's here, but I'll understand if you'd just as soon not—"

"It isn't a question of what I *want*," she said. "I have to know how it came out, although I guess there is no doubt that you executed him. The intervention of Providence-with-a-capital-*P* is greatly overrated in the lives of ordinary humans, I think. But before I take those pages . . . Paul . . ."

She stopped, as if unsure how to go on. I waited. Sometimes you can't help people. Sometimes it's better not even to try.

"Paul, you speak in here as though you had two grown children in 1932—not just one, but *two*. If you didn't get married to your Janice when you were twelve and she was eleven, something like that—"

I smiled a little. "We were young when we married—a lot of hill-people are, my own mother was—but not *that* young."

"Then how old *are* you? I've always assumed you were in your early eighties, my age, possibly even a little younger, but according to this . . ."

"I was forty the year John walked the Green Mile," I said. "I was born in 1892. That makes me a hundred and four, unless my reckoning's out."

She stared at me, speechless.

I held out the rest of the manuscript, remembering again how John had touched me, there in his cell.

You won't 'splode, he'd said, smiling a bit at the very idea, and I hadn't ... but something had happened to me, all the same. Something lasting.

"Read the rest of it," I said. "What answers I have are in there."

"All right," she almost whispered. "I'm a little afraid to, I can't lie about that, but ... all right. Where will you be?"

I stood up, stretched, listened to my spine crackle in my back. One thing that I knew for sure was that I was sick to death of the sunroom. "Out on the croquet course. There's still something I want to show you, and it's in that direction."

"Is it ... scary?" In her timid look I saw the little girl she had been back when men wore straw boaters in the summer and raccoon coats in the winter.

"No," I said, smiling. "Not scary."

"All right." She took the pages. "I'm going to take these down to my room. I'll see you out on the croquet course around ..." She riffled the manuscript, estimating. "Four? Is that all right?"

"Perfect," I said, thinking of the too-curious Brad Dolan. He would be gone by then.

She reached out, gave my arm a little squeeze, and left the room. I stood where I was for a moment, looking down at the table, taking in the fact that it was bare again except for the breakfast tray Elaine had brought me that morning, my scattered papers at last gone. I somehow couldn't believe I was done ... and as you can see, since all this was written after I recorded John Coffey's execution and gave the last batch of pages to Elaine, I was not. And even then, part of me knew why.

Alabama.

I filched the last piece of cold toast off the tray, went downstairs, and out onto the croquet course. There I sat in the sun, watching half a dozen pairs and one slow but cheerful foursome pass by waving their mallets, thinking my old man's thoughts and letting the sun warm my old man's bones.

Around two-forty-five, the three-to-eleven shift started to trickle in from the parking lot, and at three, the day-shift folks left. Most were in groups, but Brad Dolan, I saw, was walking alone. That was sort of a happy sight; maybe the world hasn't gone entirely to hell, after all. One of his joke-books was sticking out of his back pocket. The path to the parking lot goes by the croquet course, so he saw me there, but he didn't give me either a wave or a scowl. That was fine by me. He got into his old Chevrolet with the bumper sticker reading I HAVE SEEN GOD AND HIS NAME IS NEWT. Then he was gone to wherever he goes when he isn't here, laying a thin trail of discount motor oil behind.

Around four o'clock, Elaine joined me, just as she had promised. From the look of her eyes, she'd done a little more crying. She put her arms around me and hugged me tight. "Poor John Coffey," she said. "And poor Paul Edgecombe, too."

Poor Paul, I heard Jan saying. *Poor old guy.*

Elaine began to cry again. I held her, there on the croquet course in the late sunshine. Our shadows looked as if they were dancing. Perhaps in the Make-Believe Ballroom we used to listen to on the radio back in those days.

At last she got herself under control and drew back from me. She found a Kleenex in her blouse pocket and wiped her streaming eyes with it. "What happened to the Warden's wife, Paul? What happened with Melly?"

"She was considered the marvel of the age, at least by the doctors at Indianola Hospital," I said. I took her arm and we began to walk toward the path which led away from the employees' parking lot and into the woods. Toward the shed down by the wall between Georgia Pines and the world of younger people. "She died—of a heart attack, not a brain tumor—ten or eleven years later. In forty-three, I think. Hal died of a stroke right around Pearl Harbor Day—could have been *on* Pearl Harbor Day, for all

I remember—so she outlived him by two years. Sort of ironic."

"And Janice?"

"I'm not quite prepared for that today," I said. "I'll tell you another time."

"Promise?"

"Promise." But that was one I never kept. Three months after the day we walked down into the woods together (I would have held her hand, if I hadn't been afraid of hurting her bunched and swollen fingers), Elaine Connelly died quietly in her bed. As with Melinda Moores, death came as the result of a heart attack. The orderly who found her said she looked peaceful, as if it had come suddenly and without much pain. I hope he was right about that. I loved Elaine. And I miss her. Her and Janice and Brutal and just all of them.

We reached the second shed on the path, the one down by the wall. It stood back in a bower of scrub pines, its sagging roof and boarded-over windows laced and dappled with shadows. I started toward it. Elaine hung back a moment, looking fearful.

"It's all right," I said. "Really. Come on."

There was no latch on the door—there had been once, but it had been torn away—and so I used a folded-over square of cardboard to wedge it shut. I pulled it free now, and stepped into the shed. I left the door as wide open as it would go, because it was dark inside.

"Paul, what? . . . Oh. *Oh!*" That second "oh" was just shy of a scream.

There was a table pushed off to one side. On it was a flashlight and a brown paper bag. On the dirty floor was a Hav-A-Tampa cigar box I'd gotten from the concession man who refills the home's soft-drink and candy machines. I'd asked him for it special, and since his company also sells tobacco products, it was easy for him to get. I offered to pay him for it—they were valuable commodities when I worked at Cold Mountain, as I may have told you—but he just laughed me off.

Peering over the edge of it were a pair of bright little oilspot eyes.

"Mr. Jingles," I said in a low voice. "Come over here. Come on over here, old boy, and see this lady."

I squatted down—it hurt, but I managed—and held out my hand. At first I didn't think he was going to be able to get over the side of the box this time, but he made it with one final lunge. He landed on his side, then regained his feet, and came over to me. He ran with a hitching limp in one of his back legs; the injury that Percy had inflicted had come back in Mr. Jingles's old age. His old, *old* age. Except for the top of his head and the tip of his tail, his fur had gone entirely gray.

He hopped onto the palm of my hand. I raised him up and he stretched his neck out, sniffing at my breath with his ears laid back and his tiny dark eyes avid. I held my hand out toward Elaine, who looked at the mouse with wide-eyed wonder, her lips parted.

"It *can't* be," she said, and raised her eyes to me. "Oh Paul, it isn't . . . it *can't* be!"

"Watch," I said, "and then tell me that."

From the bag on the table I took a spool which I had colored myself—not with Crayolas but with Magic Markers, an invention undreamed of in 1932. It came to the same, though. It was as bright as Del's had been, maybe brighter. *Messieurs et mesdames,* I thought. *Bienvenue au cirque du mousie!*

I squatted again, and Mr. Jingles ran off my palm. He was old, but as obsessed as ever. From the moment I had taken the spool out of the bag, he'd had eyes for nothing else. I rolled it across the shed's uneven, splintery floor, and he was after it at once. He didn't run with his old speed, and his limp was painful to watch, but why should he have been either fast or surefooted? As I've said, he was old, a Methuselah of a mouse. Sixty-four, at least.

He reached the spool, which struck the far wall

and bounced back. He went around it, then lay down on his side. Elaine started forward and I held her back. After a moment, Mr. Jingles found his feet again. Slowly, so slowly, he nosed the spool back to me. When he'd first come—I'd found him lying on the steps leading to the kitchen in just that same way, as if he'd travelled a long distance and was exhausted—he had still been able to guide the spool with his paws, as he had done all those years ago on the Green Mile. That was beyond him, now; his hindquarters would no longer support him. Yet his nose was as educated as ever. He just had to go from one end of the spool to the other to keep it on course. When he reached me, I picked him up in one hand— no more than a feather, he weighed—and the spool in the other. His bright dark eyes never left it.

"Don't do it again, Paul," Elaine said in a broken voice. "I can't bear to watch him."

I understood how she felt, but thought she was wrong to ask it. He loved chasing and fetching the spool; after all the years, he still loved it just as much. We should all be so fortunate in our passions.

"There are peppermint candies in the bag, too," I said. "Canada Mints. I think he still likes them—he won't stop sniffing, if I hold one out to him—but his digestion has gotten too bad to eat them. I bring him toast, instead."

I squatted again, broke a small fragment off the piece I'd brought with me from the sunroom, and put it on the floor. Mr. Jingles sniffed at it, then picked it up in his paws and began to eat. His tail was coiled neatly around him. He finished, then looked expectantly up.

"Sometimes us old fellas can surprise you with our appetites," I said to Elaine, and handed her the toast. "You try."

She broke off another fragment and dropped it on the floor. Mr. Jingles approached it, sniffed, looked at Elaine . . . then picked it up and began to eat.

"You see?" I said. "He knows you're not a floater."

"Where did he come from, Paul?"

"Haven't a clue. One day when I went out for my early-morning walk, he was just here, lying on the kitchen steps. I knew who he was right away, but I got a spool out of the laundry room occasional basket just to be sure. And I got him a cigar box. Lined it with the softest stuff I could find. He's like us, Ellie, I think—most days just one big sore place. Still, he hasn't lost all his zest for living. He still likes his spool, and he still likes a visit from his old block-mate. Sixty years I held the story of John Coffey inside me, sixty and more, and now I've told it. I kind of had the idea that's why he came back. To let me know I should hurry up and do it while there was still time. Because I'm like him—getting there."

"Getting where?"

"Oh, you know," I said, and we watched Mr. Jingles for awhile in silence. Then, for no reason I could tell you, I tossed the spool again, even though Elaine had asked me not to. Maybe only because, in a way, him chasing a spool was like old people having their slow and careful version of sex—*you* might not want to watch it, you who are young and convinced that, when it comes to old age, an exception will be made in your case, but *they* still want to do it.

Mr. Jingles set off after the rolling spool again, clearly with pain, and just as clearly (to me, at least) with all his old, obsessive enjoyment.

"Ivy-glass windows," she whispered, watching him go.

"Ivy-glass windows," I agreed, smiling.

"John Coffey touched the mouse the way he touched you. He didn't just make you better of what was wrong with you then, he made you . . . what, resistant?"

"That's as good a word as any, I think."

"Resistant to the things that eventually bring the rest of us down like trees with termites in them. You . . . and him. Mr. Jingles. When he cupped Mr. Jingles in his hands."

"That's right. Whatever power worked through John did that—that's what I think, anyway—and now it's finally wearing off. The termites have chewed their way through our bark. It took a little longer than it does ordinarily, but they got there. I may have a few more years, men still live longer than mice, I guess, but Mr. Jingles's time is just about up."

He reached the spool, limped around it, fell over on his side, breathing rapidly (we could see his respiration moving through his gray fur like ripples), then got up and began to push it gamely back with his nose. His fur was gray, his gait was unsteady, but the oilspots that were his eyes gleamed as brightly as ever.

"You think he wanted you to write what you have written," she said. "Is that so, Paul?"

"Not Mr. Jingles," I said. "Not him but the force that—"

"Why, Paulie! And Elaine Connelly, too!" a voice cried from the open door. It was loaded with a kind of satiric horror. "As I live and breathe! What in the goodness can you two be doing here?"

I turned, not at all surprised to see Brad Dolan there in the doorway. He was grinning as a man only does when he feels he's fooled you right good and proper. How far down the road had he driven after his shift was over? Maybe only as far as The Wrangler, for a beer or two and maybe a lap-dance before coming back.

"Get out," Elaine said coldly. "Get out right now."

"Don't you tell *me* to get out, you wrinkledy old bitch," he said, still smiling. "Maybe you can tell me that up the hill, but you ain't up the hill now. This ain't where you're supposed to be. This is off-limits. Little love-nest, Paulie? Is that what you got here? Kind of a *Playboy* pad for the geriatric . . ." His eyes widened as he at last saw the shed's tenant. "What the *fuck*?"

I didn't turn to look. I knew what was there, for one thing; for another, the past had suddenly doubled over the present, making one terrible image, three-dimensional in its reality. It wasn't Brad Dolan standing there in the doorway but Percy Wetmore. In another moment he would rush into the shed and crush Mr. Jingles (who no longer had a hope of outrunning him) under his shoe. And this time there was no John Coffey to bring him back from the edge of death. Any more than there had been a John Coffey when I needed him on that rainy day in Alabama.

I got to my feet, not feeling any ache in my joints or muscles this time, and rushed toward Dolan. "Leave him alone!" I yelled. "You leave him alone, Percy, or by God I'll—"

"Who you callin Percy?" he asked, and pushed me

back so hard I almost fell over. Elaine grabbed me, although it must have hurt her to do so, and steadied me. "Ain't the first time you done it, either. And stop peein in your pants. I ain't gonna touch im. Don't need to. That's one dead rodent."

I turned, thinking that Mr. Jingles was only lying on his side to catch his breath, the way he sometimes did. He was on his side, all right, but that rippling motion through his fur had stopped. I tried to convince myself that I could still see it, and then Elaine burst into loud sobs. She bent painfully, and picked up the mouse I had first seen on the Green Mile, coming up to the duty desk as fearlessly as a man approaching his peers . . . or his friends. He lay limp on her hand. His eyes were dull and still. He was dead.

Dolan grinned unpleasantly, revealing teeth which had had very little acquaintance with a dentist. "Aw, *sakes*, now!" he said. "Did we just lose the family pet? Should we have a little funeral, with paper flowers and—"

"*SHUT UP!*" Elaine screamed at him, so loudly and so powerfully that he backed away a step, the smile slipping off his face. "*GET OUT OF HERE! GET OUT OR YOU'LL NEVER WORK ANOTHER DAY HERE! NOT ANOTHER HOUR! I SWEAR IT!*"

"You won't be able to get so much as a slice of

bread on a breadline," I said, but so low neither of them heard me. I couldn't take my eyes off Mr. Jingles, lying on Elaine's palm like the world's smallest bearskin rug.

Brad thought about coming back at her, calling her bluff—he was right, the shed wasn't exactly approved territory for the Georgia Pines inmates, even I knew that much—and then didn't. He was, at heart, a coward, just like Percy. And he might have checked on her claim that her grandson was Somebody Important and had discovered it was a true claim. Most of all, perhaps, his curiosity had been satisfied, his thirst to know slaked. And after all his wondering, the mystery had turned out not to be such of a much. An old man's pet mouse had apparently been living in the shed. Now it had croaked, had a heart attack or something while pushing a colored spool.

"Don't know why you're getting so het up," he said. "Either of you. You act like it was a *dog*, or something."

"Get out," she spat. "Get out, you ignorant man. What little mind you have is ugly and misdirected."

He flushed dully, the spots where his high school pimples had been filling in a darker red. There had been a lot of them, by the look. "I'll go," he said, "but when you come down here tomorrow ... *Paulie* ... you're going to find a new lock on this door. This place is off-limits to the residents, no matter what bad-tempered things old Mrs. My Shit Don't Stink has to say about me. Look at the floor! Boards all warped and rotted! If you was to go through, your scrawny old leg'd be apt to snap like a piece of kindling. So just take that dead mouse, if you want it, and get gone. The Love Shack is hereby closed."

He turned and strode away, looking like a man who believes he's earned at least a draw. I waited until he was gone, and then gently took Mr. Jingles from Elaine. My eyes happened on the bag with the peppermint candies in it, and that did it—the tears began to come. I don't know, I just cry easier somehow these days.

"Would you help me to bury an old friend?" I asked Elaine when Brad Dolan's heavy footsteps had faded away.

"Yes, Paul." She put her arm around my waist and laid her head against my shoulder. With one old and twisted finger, she stroked Mr. Jingles's moveless side. "I would be happy to do that."

And so we borrowed a trowel from the gardening shed and we buried Del's pet mouse as the afternoon shadows drew long through the trees, and then we walked back to get our supper and take up what remained of our lives. And it was Del I found myself thinking of, Del kneeling on the green carpet of my office with his hands folded and his bald pate gleaming in the lamplight, Del who had asked us to take care of Mr. Jingles, to make sure the bad 'un wouldn't hurt him anymore. Except the bad 'un hurts us all in the end, doesn't he?

"Paul?" Elaine asked. Her voice was both kind and exhausted. Even digging a grave with a trowel and laying a mouse to rest in it is a lot of excitement for old sweeties like us, I guess. "Are you all right?"

My arm was around her waist. I squeezed it. "I'm fine," I said.

"Look," she said. "It's going to be a beautiful sunset. Shall we stay out and watch it?"

"All right," I said, and we stayed there on the lawn for quite awhile, arms around each other's waists, first watching the bright colors come up in the sky, then watching them fade to ashes of gray.

Sainte Marie, Mère de Dieu, priez pour nous, pauvres pécheurs, maintenant et à l'heure de notre mort.

Amen.

13

1956.

Alabama in the rain.

Our third grandchild, a beautiful girl named Tessa, was graduating from the University of Florida. We went down on a Greyhound. Sixty-four, I was then, a mere stripling. Jan was fifty-nine, and as beautiful as ever. To me, at least. We were sitting in the seat all the way at the back, and she was fussing at me for not buying her a new camera to record the blessed event. I opened my mouth to tell her we had a day to shop in after we got down there, and she could have a new camera if she wanted one, it would fit the budget all right, and furthermore I thought she was just fussing because she was bored with the ride and didn't like the book she'd brought. A Perry Mason, it was. That's when everything in my memory goes white for a bit, like film that's been left out in the sun.

Do you remember that accident? I suppose a few folks reading this might, but mostly not. Yet it made front-page headlines from coast to coast when it happened. We were outside Birmingham in a driving rain, Janice complaining about her old camera, and a tire blew. The bus waltzed sideways on the wet pavement and was hit broadside by a truck hauling fertilizer. The truck slammed the bus into a bridge abutment at better than sixty miles an hour, crushed it against the concrete, and broke it in half. Two shiny, rain-streaked pieces spun in two opposite directions, the one with the diesel tank in it exploding and sending a red-black fireball up into the rainy-gray sky. At one moment Janice was complaining about her old Kodak, and at the very next I found myself lying on the far side of the underpass in the rain and staring at a pair of blue nylon panties that had spilled out of someone's suitcase. WEDNESDAY was stitched on them in black thread. There were burst-open suitcases everywhere. And bodies. And parts of bodies. There were seventy-three people on that bus, and only four survived the crash. I was one of them, the only one not seriously hurt.

I got up and staggered among the burst-open suitcases and shattered people, crying out my wife's name. I kicked aside an alarm clock, I remember that, and I remember seeing a dead boy of about thirteen lying in a strew of glass with P.F. Flyers on his feet and half his face gone. I felt the rain beating on my own face, then I went through the underpass and it was gone for awhile. When I came out on the other side it was there again, hammering my cheeks and forehead. Lying by the shattered cab of the over-turned fertilizer truck, I saw Jan. I recognized her by her red dress—it was her second-best. The best she had been saving for the actual graduation, of course.

She wasn't quite dead. I have often thought it would have been better—for me, if not for her—if she had been killed instantly. It might have made it possible for me to let her go a little sooner, a little more naturally. Or perhaps I'm only kidding myself about that. All I know for sure is that I have *never* let her go, not really.

She was trembling all over. One of her shoes had come off and I could see her foot jittering. Her eyes were open but blank, the left one full of blood, and as I fell on my knees next to her in the smoky-smelling rain, all I could think of was that jitter meant she was being electrocuted; she was being electrocuted and I had to hold the roll before it was too late.

"Help me!" I screamed. "Help me, someone help me!"

No one helped, no one even came. The rain pounded down—a hard, soaking rain that flattened my still-black hair against my skull—and I held her in my arms and no one came. Her blank eyes looked up at me with a kind of dazed intensity, and blood poured from the back of her crushed head in a freshet. Beside one trembling, mindlessly spasming hand was a piece of chromed steel with the letters GREY on it. Next to that was roughly one quarter of what had once been a businessman in a brown wool suit.

"Help me!" I screamed again, and turned toward the underpass, and there I saw John Coffey standing in the shadows, only a shadow himself, a big man with long, dangling arms and a bald head. *"John!"* I screamed. *"Oh John, please help me! Please help Janice!"*

Rain ran into my eyes. I blinked it away, and he was gone. I could see the shadows I had mistaken for John . . . but it hadn't been *only* shadows. I'm sure of that. He was there. Maybe only as a ghost, but he was there, the rain on his face mixing with the endless flow of his tears.

She died in my arms, there in the rain beside that fertilizer truck with the smell of burning diesel fuel in my nose. There was no moment of awareness— the eyes clearing, the lips moving in some whispered final declaration of love. There was a kind of shivery clench in the flesh beneath my hands, and then she was gone. I thought of Melinda Moores for the first time in years, then, Melinda sitting up in the bed where all the doctors at Indianola General Hospital had believed she would die; Melinda Moores looking fresh and rested and peering at John Coffey with bright, wondering eyes. Melinda saying *I dreamed you were wandering in the dark, and so was I. We found each other.*

I put my wife's poor, mangled head down on the wet pavement of the interstate highway, got to my feet (it was easy; I had a little cut on the side of my left hand, but that was all), and screamed his name into the shadows of the underpass.

"John! JOHN COFFEY! WHERE ARE YOU, BIG BOY?"

I walked toward those shadows, kicking aside a teddy-bear with blood on its fur, a pair of steel-rimmed eyeglasses with one shattered lens, a severed hand with a garnet ring on the pinky finger. *"You saved Hal's wife, why not my wife? Why not Janice? WHY NOT MY JANICE?"*

No answer; only the smell of burning diesel and burning bodies, only the rain falling ceaselessly out of the gray sky and drumming on the cement while my wife lay dead on the road behind me. No answer then and no answer now. But of course it wasn't only Melly Moores that John Coffey saved in 1932, or Del's mouse, the one that could do that cute trick with the spool and seemed to be looking for Del long before Del showed up . . . long before John Coffey showed up, either.

John saved me, too, and years later, standing in the pouring Alabama rain and looking for a man who wasn't there in the shadows of an underpass, standing amid the spilled luggage and the ruined dead, I learned a terrible thing: sometimes there is absolutely no difference at all between salvation and damnation.

I felt one or the other pouring through me as we sat together on his bunk—November the eighteenth, nineteen and thirty-two. Pouring out of him and into me, whatever strange force he had in him coming through our joined hands in a way our love and hope and good intentions somehow never can, a feeling that began as a tingle and then turned into something tidal and enormous, a force beyond anything I had ever experienced before or have ever experienced since. Since that day I have never had pneumonia, or the flu, or even a strep throat. I have never had another urinary infection, or so much as an infected cut. I have had colds, but they have been infrequent—six or seven years apart, and although people who don't have colds often are supposed to suffer more serious ones, that has never been the case with me. Once, earlier on in that awful year of 1956, I passed a gallstone. And although I suppose it will sound strange to some reading this in spite of all I have said, part of me relished the pain that came when that gallstone went. It was the only serious pain I'd had since that problem with my waterworks, twenty-four years before. The ills that have taken my friends and same-generation loved ones until there are none of them left—the strokes, the cancers, the heart attacks, the liver diseases, the blood diseases—have all left me untouched, have swerved to avoid me the way a man driving a car swerves to avoid a deer or a raccoon in the road. The one serious accident I was in left me untouched save for a scratch on the hand. In 1932, John Coffey inoculated me with life. *Electrocuted* me with life, you might say. I will pass on eventually—of course I will, any illusions of immortality I might have had died with Mr. Jingles—but I will have wished for death long before death finds me. Truth to tell, I wish for it already and have ever since Elaine Connelly died. Need I tell you?

I look back over these pages, leafing through them with my trembling, spotted hands, and I wonder if there is some meaning here, as in those books which are supposed to be uplifting and ennobling. I think back to the sermons of my childhood, booming affirmations in the church of Praise Jesus, The Lord Is Mighty, and I recall how the preachers used to say that God's eye is on the sparrow, that He sees and marks even the least of His creations. When I think of Mr. Jingles, and the tiny scraps of wood we found in that hole in the beam, I think that is so. Yet this same God sacrificed John Coffey, who tried only to do good in his blind way, as savagely as any Old Testament prophet ever sacrificed a defenseless lamb . . . as Abraham would have sacrificed his own son if actually called upon to do so. I think of John saying that Wharton killed the Detterick twins with their love for each other, and that it happens every day, all over the world. If it happens, God *lets* it happen, and when we say "I don't understand," God replies, "I don't care."

I think of Mr. Jingles dying while my back was turned and my attention usurped by an unkind man whose finest emotion seemed to be a species of vindictive curiosity. I think of Janice, jittering away her last mindless seconds as I knelt with her in the rain.

Stop it, I tried to tell John that day in his cell. *Let go of my hands, I'm going to drown if you don't. Drown or explode.*

"You won't 'splode," he answered, hearing my thought and smiling at the idea. And the horrible thing is that I didn't. I haven't.

I have at least one old man's ill: I suffer from insomnia. Late at night I lie in my bed, listening to the dank and hopeless sound of infirm men and women coughing their courses deeper into old age. Sometimes I hear a call-bell, or the squeak of a shoe in the corridor, or Mrs. Javits's little TV tuned to the late news. I lie here, and if the moon is in my window, I watch it. I lie here and think about Brutal, and Dean, and sometimes William Wharton saying *That's right, nigger, bad as you'd want.* I think of Delacroix saying *Watch this Boss Edgecombe, I teach Mr. Jingles a new trick.* I think of Elaine, standing in the door of the sunroom and telling Brad Dolan to leave me alone. Sometimes I doze and see that underpass in the rain, with John Coffey standing beneath it in the shadows. It's never just a trick of the eye, in these little dreams; it's always him for sure, my big boy, just standing there and watching. I lie here and wait. I think about Janice, how I lost her, how she ran away red through my fingers in the rain, and I wait. We each owe a death, there are no exceptions, I know that, but sometimes, oh God, the Green Mile is so long.

Author's Afterword

I don't think I'd want to do another serial novel (if only because the critics get to kick your ass six times instead of just the once), but I wouldn't have missed the experience for the world. As I write this afterword on the day before Part 2 of *The Green Mile* is to be published, the serialization experiment is looking like a success, at least in terms of sales. For that, Constant Reader, I want to thank you. And something a bit different wakes us all up a little, maybe—lets us see the old business of storytelling in a new way. That's how it worked for me, anyway.

I wrote in a hurry because the format demanded that I write in a hurry. That was part of the exhilaration, but it also may have produced a number of anachronisms. The guards and prisoners listen to *Allen's Alley* on their E Block radio, and I doubt if Fred Allen was actually broadcasting in 1932. The same may hold true for Kay Kyser and his *Kollege of Musical Knowledge.* This isn't to let me off the hook, but it sometimes seems to me that history which has recently fallen over the horizon is harder to research than the Middle Ages or the time of the Crusades. I was able to determine that Brutal might indeed have called the mouse on the Mile Steamboat Willy—the Disney cartoon had been in existence almost four years by then—but I have a sneaking suspicion that the little pornographic comic book featuring Popeye and Olive Oyl is an artifact out of time. I might clean up some of this stuff when and if I decide to do *The Green Mile* as a single volume . . . but maybe I'll leave the goofs. After all, doesn't the great Shakespeare himself include in *Julius Caesar* the anachronism of a striking clock long before mechanical clocks were invented?

Doing *The Green Mile* as a single volume would present its own unique challenges, I have come to realize, partly because the book couldn't be published as it was issued in its installments. Because I took Charles Dickens as my model, I asked several people how Dickens had handled the problem of refreshing his readers' recollections at the beginning of each new episode. I had expected something like the synopses which preceded each installment of my beloved *Saturday Evening Post* serials, and discovered that Dickens had not been so crude; he built the synopsis into the actual story.

While I was trying to decide how to do this, my wife began telling me (she doesn't exactly nag, but sometimes she *advocates* rather ruthlessly) that I had never really finished the story of Mr. Jingles, the circus mouse. I thought she was right, and began to see that, by making Mr. Jingles a secret of Paul Edgecombe's in his old age, I could create a fairly interesting "front story." (The result is a little bit like the form taken by the film version of *Fried Green Tomatoes*.) In fact, everything in Paul's front story—the story of his life at the Georgia Pines old folks' home—turned out to my satisfaction. I particularly liked the way that Dolan, the orderly, and Percy Wetmore became entwined in Paul's mind. And that was not something I planned or did on purpose; like the happiest of fictions, it just ambled along and stepped into its place.

I want to thank Ralph Vicinanza for bringing me the "serial thriller" idea in the first place, and all my friends at Viking Penguin and Signet for getting behind it, even though they were scared to death at the beginning (all writers are crazy, and of course they knew that). I also want to thank Marsha DeFilippo, who transcribed a whole stenographer's notebook full of my cramped handwriting and never complained. Well ... *rarely* complained.

Most of all, though, I want to thank my wife, Tabitha, who read this story and said she liked it. Writers almost always write with some ideal reader in mind, I think, and my wife is mine. We don't always see eye to eye when it comes to what we each write (hell, we rarely see eye to eye when we're shopping together in the supermarket), but when she says it's good, it usually is. Because she's tough, and if I try to cheat or cut a corner, she always sees it.

And you, Constant Reader. Thank you, as well, and if you have any ideas about *The Green Mile* as a single volume, please let me know.

—Stephen King
April 28, 1996
New York City

COMPETITION NO.6
THE FINAL CHALLENGE

WIN A MASSIVE
6,000
AIR MILES AWARDS
THE SKY REALLY IS THE LIMIT!!!

Plus a complete set of *The Green Mile*, signed by
Stephen King.

see next page for details

WIN 6,000 AIR MILES AWARDS

plus a complete set of *The Green Mile*
signed by Stephen King

0881 88 77 66

Call the above number with your answers to the following
questions and you could escape to a fantastic destination of
your choice. The sky is the limit!!!!

1. Who was the central character throughout
   The Green Mile?
2. How many people were electrocuted on
   'Old Sparky' during *The Green Mile*?
3. Who was the real murderer of Cora and
   Kathe?

Telephone lines close MIDNIGHT 31 OCTOBER 1996

TERMS AND CONDITIONS